JELLYFISH HAVE NO EARS

ADÈLE ROSENFELD

JELLYFISH HAVE
NO EARS

Translated from the French by
Jeffrey Zuckerman

MACLEHOSE PRESS
QUERCUS · LONDON

First published as *Les méduses n'ont pas d'oreilles* by Grasset, Paris, in 2022
First published in Great Britain in 2024 by

MacLehose Press
An imprint of Quercus Publishing Ltd
Carmelite House, 50 Victoria Embankment, London EC4Y 0DZ

An Hachette UK company

  Supported using public funding by
ARTS COUNCIL ENGLAND

This book has been selected to receive financial assistance from English PEN's
PEN Translates programme, supported by Arts Council England. English PEN exists
to promote literature and our understanding of it, to uphold writers' freedoms
around the world, to campaign against the persecution and imprisonment
of writers for stating their views, and to promote the friendly co-operation of
writers and the free exchange of ideas. www.englishpen.org

ISBN (PB) 978 1 52943 791 1
ISBN (Ebook) 978 1 52943 792 8

10 9 8 7 6 5 4 3 2 1

Designed and typeset in Sabon by Libanus Press Ltd
Printed and bound in Great Britain by Clays Ltd, Elcograf S.p.A.

Papers used by MacLehose Press are
from well-managed forests and other
responsible sources.

"Language can arguably only be entered through what is indescribable. And what is indecipherable. The entrance is neither within nor without. Nowhere to be found and yet there. Through what is imperceptible, we are utterly, smilingly complicit."
Thierry Metz, *L'Homme qui penche*

"Every word is a hole, an abyss, a trap."
Ghérasim Luca

I

It was the Castaigne building. What I'd heard was Castagne. Before I went through double doors that swung like in an old Western, there was a small sign saying OTO-RHINO-LARYNGOLOGY (ORL) and HEAD & NECK SURGERY, IMPLANT SERVICES. Only otorhinolaryngology was familiar to me. When I was little, I thought it was a sub-branch of rhinoceros studies.

In my ears were muted thumps, the drumbeat of my pulse. I took a seat at the end of the hallway, next to a table covered with magazines about deafness, one of them offering up anecdotes about isolation in the workplace. I glanced up after each line so I wouldn't miss my name being called and saw that an old woman in a wheelchair had parked across from me, right by the magazine *For the Deaf*. On the cover, text in a box read "Language can be reassuring or restrictive: people think that complicating blunt words softens them. They're ashamed to say *deaf, blind, old, has a mental disorder*: there's a slippery slope from *hard-of-hearing* and *critical cases* by way of *vision-impaired* and *senior citizen* to *the dead* being called *the unliving.*" When I realised that the old woman – or *senior citizen*, or *elderly person*, whatever I ought to call her – was shouting at me, I interrupted: "Ma'am, I don't think I hear any better than you do," but she didn't understand and kept on with her croaky monologue.

A man put an end to the one-sided conversation: "Come with me, please." I followed him into the padded room; he shut the door behind me, gripping a huge chrome-metal handle that struck me in its similarity to butchers' cold rooms – except what was being carved up here, meticulously, slice by thin slice, was sound. He set the headphones on my ears, delicately, as if he were placing electrodes on a chicken's head, and handed me a joystick. The first sounds came through, but not all; some merely pulsed against my eardrum.

Then it was time for the words, I had to repeat the list like a messed-up parrot. Most of it was absurd and I had to resist letting my imagination fill the gaps.

> woman
> lemon
> boulder
> soldier
> poppy
> button
> blacksmith
> apron
> shoulder

The deep voice ran through the words, which grew muffled one by one and faded into fog. To fend off the sharpening mirages, my mind chased in the half-darkness after these words: they were my stronghold against the widening craters of language being shelled. I was used to rambling amid silences and lost words, letting pure imagination buoy me, but the words at this point were so faint that what reality remained was akin to a ravaged landscape, giving the few images now emerging all the more vividness. This was a past world: a husband home from the war, from so many dead bodies, rediscovering a forgotten space. I could see his face in the slanting light; he was there naming things in a flat voice to reclaim the life he'd had. He said "woman" and his eyes fell on his wife's head of curls as she sobbed silently, then his eyes turned to the fruit basket and he said "lemon", and then his face tilted up to the window and the craggy Brittany shore, and he designated it with his mouth: "boulder". And he recalled the life he'd returned from: "soldier", and all the seasons he'd spent in that role. He said "poppy" while looking at that flower swaying between her and him, now split open. He looked down to hide his misty eyes and uttered "button", his uniform reminding him of all those other soldiers. His lips whispered "blacksmith"; his eyes were dead, but his lips went on whispering something his wife didn't hear, "apron" – the blacksmith always kept with him a scrap of fabric from this woman he loved.

The soldier couldn't hold back his growing smile, until he said "shoulder", loud enough to startle the woman who looked at him with concern, recalling the shoulders of the other soldiers torn apart by heavy artillery.

"Now we're going to do the left," the audiologist said, pointing to my other ear. The story of the soldier reverberated in my deaf ear. The sounds that crashed against the dead eardrum were the soundtrack of his memories. The lingering trace of words was reduced to a presence.

I sat once again in the chair that faced the office to assess the damage on the audiogram. I took careful note of the concave curve on the paper, a tight grid of x and y lines quantifying the remaining sound. It was like a bird's-eye view of the Normandy coast: the tide of silence was now covering more than half the page.

2

In the ORL specialist's office, cutaway diagrams of the inner ear brightened the room with hues of red and blue. The outer ear was displayed in an unremarkable pink whereas the inner ear was by turns sand yellow, carmine red and pinkish beige, culminating in an ultramarine labyrinth: the cochlea. What it really looked like was an overcooked Burgundy snail.

The doctor sat down at her desk, her hands clutching the folder with all my audiograms, and overenunciated her words. It doesn't bode well when a doctor who specialises in implants looks at your latest audiogram and then talks to you like you're an idiot. I wasn't feeling so good now.

"You've effectively lost fifteen decibels. That's a lot."

I told her how it had happened, or rather how it hadn't happened.

No warning signs – although what signs would have come and warned?

It had withered away, simple as that.

Well, actually, there were two specific times when I realised that the sound was gone.

The first was early August, while I was having a coffee in London, and the waiter spoke to me. He stood there, his lips moving but no sound coming. I stammered in broken English, saying that I didn't understand, not a thing. The distress was clear on my face. He responded – well, I think I got a response from his lips and the words parting them – that I spoke bad English. I lost the soundtrack there, in the city of London. Somewhere between Churchway and Stoneway, the tide ebbed.

The second was in Brittany. I'd gone to see a friend at Plougrescant, and as we were having dinner, the sound cut out again. I saw his white hair and his mouth stretching into a smile, the corners of his lips bracketing a story that the wind bore away. The silence turned leaden. I could make out "Brazil", so he had to be talking about his conference. I laughed so he wouldn't catch on.

All I told the doctor was: "It happened gradually, in August."

She replied that a hospital stay to undergo a procedure was essential, but it wouldn't be a sure thing. And then there was another solution: a cochlear implant. She thought an implant on the right, the ear that still worked, would be better; with the left ear, it would just be an unintelligible mess. I needed to understand that, after a long stretch of rehabilitation, between six months and a year, my hearing at every frequency would improve. The operation, however, was irreversible: the "natural" hearing I currently had would be lost.

The few cilia remaining deep in my ear caught high pitches and a few low ones, which barely allowed me to reconstruct the meaning of what I heard. What I really still got was a sense of the warmth of timbres, this soft sheen of wind, of colour, of all sound's snags and snarls.

I looked at the grey-and-blue knobs of plastic, those scale models of implants sitting on her desk. They could have been fridge magnets.

I didn't know what else to say. She held out her hand. I gripped it, feeling like I was clinging to any branch I could.

3

I made my way to room 237 so the secretary could give me the paperwork, then to the Babinski building, named after an early-twentieth-century neurologist. His portrait was by the entrance, with a small enamel plaque: JOSEPH BABINSKI (1857–1932).

I learned that he was mainly known for a neurological exam that consisted of stroking the arch of grown-ups' and babies' feet. His concept of pithiatism (from the Greek πείθειν, *to persuade*) was less famous but still had a huge impact on many soldiers after World War I. Shell shock was, at the time, an unknown phenomenon. In the vein of Professor Jean-Martin Charcot, the father of neurology, Babinski had defined a new form of hysteria: many of the men to return from war suffered from issues that, lacking a clear causal relationship, remained orphaned.

Orphaned.

Yes, that was very much how I'd always felt, this sensation of not belonging to any community. Not deaf enough to be a part of Deaf culture, not hearing enough to be fully within the hearing world. It all came down to what I'd convinced myself to be or not be. The collateral damage that had chipped away at my self-worth and my confidence were, for those soldiers, orphaned issues that they struggled to make sense of. Did the void in me come from that? An absence that had to be filled by excess?

"With you, things are *tout noir ou tout blanc*," I was always told. Wholly black or white. But I kept hearing it as "*trou noir*". Black hole.

"You hear what you want to hear."

How could I have convinced them otherwise?

But this was perfectly real, and the hospital was shining a light on the hole at the centre of it all.

My mother was beside me, staring at the newspaper. She pointed at the front page: "Look, it's the first photo of a black hole."

4

The room was on the third floor. I could leave my belongings there; I had a full schedule and a procedure to undergo. A nurse came to ask me slightly odd questions, such as my morning routine: Bath or shower? Jacuzzi, please.

The nurse left me there, befuddled, then so did my mother. I still couldn't really believe that my ears had landed me here. I'd tried so hard to get them to keep this secret, only for them to squeal on me and trap me within these four white walls to reckon with my past.

I'd tried to manage things as best I could after so many years of denial then so many years of fighting that denial, contorting my life one way then another, but this loss had blown everything to pieces.

The door opened and a nurse by the name of Eddy came in to puncture my eardrum and inject a fluid directly into my auditory organ. The anaesthetic was pointless, nothing more than a procedure to carry out so that patients believed that something was being done. But when I saw the needle, I couldn't believe it. He was going to stick *that* into my ear? I could feel my eardrum puckering like an oyster that had just had lemon squeezed on it.

The hospital stay also involved seeing a psychologist, a tall woman with sad eyes. She waved elegantly for me to sit in a chair facing her and explained that this meeting was an informal conversation to assess my prospects as a hard-of-hearing person. I gave her the bullet points of my career: a practically spotless academic record and a degree without any help.

The psychologist took down all this information, looking serious, and sketched out a summary, repeating herself any time I furrowed my brow. I'd worked so hard to adapt that I had to be on the verge of collapse; dealing with this new degree of hearing loss might well revive old spectres of trauma.

I wasn't alone on that front, she went on, all hard-of-hearing individuals went through bouts of depression, a result of the cumulative effort that hearing society didn't see. It's hard to measure this effort and it's not easy for friends and family to understand this, or any other invisible disability. Those who are hard-of-hearing have a tendency, at times, to cut themselves off from other people.

At the sight of my face consumed with questions, she suddenly shifted to a reassuring tone: "There are solutions, and one of them is a cochlear implant."

"But with an implant I won't hear the way I did before."

"Your brain will have forgotten what 'before' means."

Then she added: "It's true that there's a sense of mourning. Something's lost, yes. But there's no knowing what, in turn, might be found."

5

The hospital stay was dependent upon my file's continued existence. Documents were added to it, but nobody read them; it was merely a prop to justify my presence. My days were a long string of pop quizzes that somehow left the quizzers no less quizzical. "What are you here for?" "How long has your stay been?" "What procedure are you undergoing?": a morass of faces asked me a morass of questions because they didn't read the file.

My file got lost, but I was told not to miss any of my appointments. "Which ones?" I asked. "My colleague will get back to you about that." Except they were all colleagues and not a single one bothered to get back to me about that.

My trust in medical institutions was crumbling. I hated the doctors doing grand rounds with a gaggle of medical students trailing behind like crabby teenagers being dragged through pouring rain on a field trip to Dieppe.

Everything was weighing on me: within the room's confines I was an ailing woman, a future implant recipient. The one place away from prying eyes was the chapel, a seventeenth-century edifice shaped like a Greek cross, hidden within the hospital grounds. I generally steered clear of such religious spaces, but every other room had already let me down. The chapel was under the patronage of Saint Rita, an Augustinian nun and the patroness of impossible causes. I could pray to her. I wrote a note for her, even though I knew she wouldn't be reading my file either.

Each day I dragged my IV drip to the chapel, the stand's wheels clattering on the stones. Then I made my way, in a slow, silent procession, with my metallic pole for a shepherd's rod, to the Babinski building. And each fluorescent-lit night, back in my room, I chewed my bland food.

I dreamed that my soldier was tucking me in while I slept, singing a song with no consonants. Saint Rita twirled her skirts layered like a nesting doll to fend off the cold. The consonant-less song disappeared amid the snow, the bass line crackled, the vowels snuffed out at the snowflakes' least touch.

I never heard the door open in the morning even though the nurse yelled before entering. The nurses seemed annoyed. Even in the ORL ward, not hearing was still a class war with the hearing.

On the last day, I had an appointment with a specialist so I could be released: "There haven't been any conclusive results," she pronounced as she handed over a folder thick with appointments.

As I made my way down hallways, up paths, and across the lawn towards the exit, I tried to get my mind around my silence-future.

6

I returned to civilian life and my neighbourhood struck me as being like a stage set, almost unreal with its blocky buildings and narrow roads. The roots of the trees burst through the asphalt up and down the avenues. It was October and the chestnut trees were all skin and bones already.

"You're back," my neighbour-friend exclaimed. "Let's get drinks and celebrate!"

Standing in my flat, it felt so nice to pull soft clothes onto my body hurting all over, and I spun around so I could feel like my room was mine and mine alone again. All the sounds clumped together and stretched out as in one of those anamorphic drawings: the ambulance in the street and the toilet flush merging into a single streak of sound with shrill points.

I got to the restaurant, where the neighbour-friend was waiting for me; his cheek-kiss and his round voice pushed away the hubbub. I clung to his words ringed by high notes. When my eyes weren't locked on his lips, his voice seemed warm, its contours sharp like a solar eclipse. The middle-register core was inaudible, but its luminous edges formed by the higher tones allowed me to grasp the meaning. I managed to follow almost everything he was telling me, which made me happy. We laughed in the night about returning to the world. For a second, he was serious again.

He was telling me about an architect in Japan, about the concrete church he'd erected with its massive cross carved in the chancel's wall, not unlike a window: the outside light cast its shape throughout. I couldn't help thinking of how this image matched the one I had of his voice: sharp high notes bright with the light of meaning, set off against the heavy, grey vocal range of the middle registers.

"Tadao Ando!" he blurted out.

And at my puzzlement, he clarified:

"Tadao Ando is the name of the architect I was telling you about."

His huge blue eyes were smiling, and mine were, too. Our drinks made the language being gutted by my cilia-less ears reel and sway. His boozy breath recalled the odour of antiseptic. I must have had too many artichokes. He didn't like them and had pushed them all my way. And he was starting to get delightfully sloshed, too, his words drifting off and his eyes filling with lust. After eight days at the hospital, this rowdy meal with a man was getting the better of me. Suddenly he looked terribly sad; I saw the bluish halo of the circles under his eyes. There was some-thing of Turner in the colouring around his gaze, his blue eyes like a sailboat violently adrift in his anxiety. For a second I thought I was looking at my soldier.

His form appeared behind the neighbour-friend, the curls of their hair intertwined, my soldier's black curls practically the shadow of my neighbour-friend's pale curls.

"What are you looking at?"

My eyes returned to his lips churning up a whirlwind of words, and his tongue swinging like a bell's clapper.

What was he talking about? Between the two of us sitting there, the words escaped me. The various parts of his body provided no clarification, but I could sense desire surging up. His hands were driving home the thrust of the story, hammering the point home but not revealing a thing. His eyes were no help either and that was actually what I hated most: they were only checking to see if I understood. Thankfully, my own eyes weren't blue – well, that was one advantage I'd always had in life. With my jet-black eyes I could douse the phatic function of language, its social role. At least in the darkness there was nothing to plumb. With my dark eyes, I could feel safe; the other person would never know whether or not I understood. With my dark eyes, I could plug every crack, I could double-check every detail.

There was a chalkboard on which I was the hangman: "F _ _ _ SH _ D?" the waiter was asking me.

Given the state of my plate, he probably wanted to clear it. What could the waiter be asking me in a single word? My soldier's massive hands formed a cross as a clue: done? It had to be a longer synonym. Too late, the neighbour-friend answered for me and the plate was gone. The dark curls disappeared, my soldier vanished.

Once we were outside, my confusion cleared up in the quiet of the winter street, and the neighbour-friend's voice felt all-encompassing again. Our bodies walked in lock-step, our strides slipping into sync amid the darkness and our drunkenness.

By his door, in our building's courtyard, I felt a new kinship with him, and as his lips brushed mine, I became a sensuous fruit to be squeezed by his arms.

The light or brown curls shook free amid the bedsheets, coiled around my fingers, my nipples. But the desire driving us to retrace those paths that so many bodies had trod before soon proved too meagre to be called love. My eyes lingered on the man curled up in sleep until I, too, finally slipped into slumber.

7

In the morning, the bed was cold. It took me some time to realise where I was, and only then did I grope around on the floor for my piled-up belongings. Except, grabbing at the hem of my pants, I caught the sleeve of the soldier's blue greatcoat; my sweater lay atop his trousers and the puttees had unrolled into the hallway where his cap and boots still were.

I just couldn't shake off the hospital.

Back in my flat, I clung desperately to those last sensations, but even inside me all that remained was a wide field of poppies.

In the days that followed, I didn't see either my soldier or the neighbour-friend. Whether it was me steering clear or them avoiding me, I couldn't tell.

I lay low, listless, mapping my silence-future in the reassuring confines of walls I had chosen, not yet brave enough to face the outside world and its alien hubbub.

The street's noises were a featureless hum. Nothing stood out from the shapeless mass. Before, I'd been able to discern layers; now, everything was flattened out.

"Ever since you were little, you've been walking a tightrope, keeping your balance between two worlds, neither of which you entirely belong in, and the minute you put a foot wrong, like you're doing now that you have fifteen decibels less, you fall and you have to learn how to hear all over again," my speech therapist explained to my wan face. At least I could still understand his perfectly pitched voice.

Outside had become a source of anxiety, but I had to reprovision the flat in which I'd sequestered myself. At the supermarket, the voices blurred into a single echo. An epidemic of sorts had spread across all sound: the jam jars that the stock boy was shelving chattered; the product codes' beeps at the checkout seeped into the women's stressed syllables like fantastical outbursts; the deli-counter machine let out a hoarse cough. At the checkout, I over-heard "bulgur" or maybe "burur". To a "you" – *static* – "there", I answered yes twice without understanding, replied no three times without understanding, and finally declared "I don't know," still without understanding. Tensions mounted. I paid and left, both of us feeling fed up.

Later on I would learn that the staticky phenomenon had a name: psychoacoustic distortion. The brain, not yet having internalised the loss of middle-low frequencies, functioned more or less like a TV on a stormy day.

In the evening, my bedroom was filled with an odd

sound. Abrupt, random thuds against a guttural background followed me until I fell into deep sleep. During one of my sleepless bouts of pacing, the soldier turned up again, in the corner of the room, playing with a cup-and-ball, the ball managing to land about half the time in the cup which he gripped tight. He let out a guttural "mmm" sound. It occurred to me that he, too, might be toying with language through this game, that he was practising getting the *ah* in the *uh* with the cup-and-ball.

Sometimes, the ball hitting the ground woke me up at night, or in the morning, and when I opened my eyes, the last wisps of smoke from the soldier's cigarette would be swirling into the morning's haze.

"I hear weird sounds at night," I told the speech therapist.

"That's tinnitus."

"But there's also shaking, I'd say about a magnitude three on the Richter scale."

"Could that be the neighbours' washing machine during the spin cycle?"

8

I didn't suffer any visitors, apart from my mother, who wanted to make sure I was still more or less alive. Not only was I getting lost every time she shifted between her middle register and her higher tones, my eyes were losing focus with exhaustion and the words were changing shape on her lips.

Lips moving haltingly, eyes wide – "bear" – *lips smacking, eyes indicating pleasure* – "forest, it was delicious."

I nodded without understanding, and went along with the image of my mother walking through the forest, most likely by her friend's place in the Pyrénées. I imagined her relishing the pleasure of being alive, and doing so even though bears had been newly reintroduced into the region.

My eyes managed to regain focus on her lips. "Have you tried any yourself?" she was asking.

"Tried what, Maman? Walking through the forest?"

I prayed for the light not to change, for the clouds to stay put, so as not to ruin the perfect view of my mother's lips as she sat on the sofa.

"No, bear's garlic, have you tried any, I bought some

at" – a cloud passed, I lost my grip on the vowels, it was now nothing more than a succession of *b*'s, *t*'s, and *d*'s, maybe even *f*'s, and then the sun came back. "Well, batteries who hold just how to fake up in the methods."

Fake up in the methods. Well, that wasn't something I cared about enough to keep paying attention.

"Why aren't you listening?" she asked, annoyed.

"Methods, who wants to talk about that?"

It was her turn to stare in befuddlement.

I hadn't picked the topic, and clearly neither had she. It was all mere chance. So, who was stacking the cards of conversation then?

9

In the following days, I stayed put to orient my body towards silence. Holding it up like a sheet to the light, to get to grips with all the registers of sound. In the intervening nights, I kept returning to a ritual I'd had since I was little: rubbing my ear against the pillow. Making a personal audiogram, gauging my hearing amid my fears of going totally deaf. Deaf and blind in the darkness. The pillow-gauge always made the same sound, of crepe paper, which was comforting. But now the pillow wasn't crinkling the way it used to. The sound had grown distant, low; where it had once been so sharp and distinct, it had faded to grey.

Signs of worry emerged. I wound my hair around my fingers and, as this tic became more compulsive, one day a dialogue began:

"Did you really think getting rid of me would fix things?"

My hair was still mad at me for shaving it off ten years ago.

"We've been over this. I thought it would help, that shaving you off would make my disability visible."

"You took such good care of me, and then, overnight, you cut me into a thousand pieces."

"I wanted them to see what I had on my ear, see that things were tricky for me."

The hair kept whining, annoyed: "Just wait until you get cancer, then you'll actually feel bad about what you did."

I stopped stroking it.

Even with my head shaved, nothing had changed. People hadn't been any more understanding about my disability when they could see my hearing aid.

I felt like I'd been plopped down, without any instructions or guidance, in a society that needed me to be exactly like every other citizen and find my place and do my job.

Sometimes I glimpsed the worried soldier moving like a shadow, stumbling. Sometimes I even sensed his dazed eyes on me. Twice a day, he brought me a bowl of broth, always the same thin broth. All it took was a glimpse of his mad eyes to tell he wasn't quite all there. He brought his shaky hand to the box of KUB OR bouillon cubes and, with his lunatic gaze, watered the mixture down. He wasn't happy.

I stayed cooped up in the silence, while the soldier fixated on KUB cubes, stirring the brownish soup endlessly. The noise of the whisk against the pot clattered off the walls like an army being soundly defeated, battering my own silent withdrawal.

I set my hand on his shoulder to bring him back

to earth, but as neither he nor I seemed to be in any semblance of reality, he kept on clanging away.

Some time ago, I read that the fear of an enemy invasion had set off a wave of mental disorders, driving soldiers to desert before leaving for the front lines. A battalion commander had even developed a paranoid obsession due to rumours about these very KUB bouillon cubes. In 1914, ads for the German-sounding brand had been put up on street corners, at intersections, and rumour had it that they were signposts directing the invading troops towards Paris.

I tried to soothe the soldier by exhaling softly on his neck, stroking him quietly, steering him away from defeat, from the sounds of greatcoats and bandoliers, the enemy's insanity. He slowed his hand, then stopped beating his fury.

I meditated, my eyes shut. In my head this mirrored the war that had broken out anew between my two halves, the one deaf and the other hearing. I was used to the darkness of silence, but I couldn't forget about the part of me that was hearing.

It was time to go outside.

I took up the reins of my existence, I shook off those KUB bouillon cubes and started looking for work. As I flooded the job market with CVs labelled "Verified Disabled Applicant", the soldier smoked in the sunshine.

The first positive response I got was for a short-term contract at the local government office. The job description was a bit vague, but then again, so were my background and aims.

After some emails, I had an interview with the woman who was probably the division head. On the day of, terrified that I might not understand something and get stage fright, I reviewed how I was going to present myself. How could I answer questions about meetings, about talking on the phone? I had no idea anymore what I was or wasn't capable of.

The government offices for the arrondissement were in a building thirty minutes by bus from my flat: an annexe between two Haussmann structures that stood out for its glass door and its façade alternating between drywall and panes of coated and tinted glass. Once I was past security,

I found myself in a small room that, with its blue plastic seats bolted together and its fake banana tree, looked like a tiny rural train station. A tall, pale woman with round shoulders came to get me, gave me a limp handshake, and told me to follow her.

As I walked behind her, I sensed that she was talking to me, her nasal voice getting lost amid its echoes against the walls. I couldn't bring myself to explain the situation, feeling more comfortable offering a stupid smile that she glimpsed as she looked back to make sure I was still there. I had no idea whether what she'd said warranted an answer, if she'd already formed an opinion of me or if she hadn't noticed, but when I entered her office, the tension was palpable.

I sat down in the chair across from her and took in the piles of folders that amounted to a moat between us. Unfortunately for me, her head was buried behind the computer warming me with its whirring fan, which didn't help matters any.

"Well, you" – I contorted myself to make out her lips but the pale face shifted out of sight. "Summer."

Was she talking about a job just for the summer? Well, why not.

Was she asking me if I'd gone anywhere this summer? That couldn't be right.

Was she wondering if I'd had a nice summer? There was no sense in that.

Maybe she'd said "paper" rather than "summer", in which case she could have started the interview by asking if I had a printout of my CV.

I took my chances and answered yes.

Her brunette head emerged from behind the screen and eyed me in surprise, before retreating back into its hideaway.

Then I thought I could make out, amid the throat-clearing or groaning, the word "pretentious". My memory of phonemes turned up no other possibilities. Was I the subject of that adjective? What could I possibly say to something so mean-spirited? What did she mean?

Anger rose in me, while the groans only got even louder.

The voice behind the computer asked, "You do know that" – *yipping* – "we" – *groaning*.

All I heard now was barking, grunting, yipping, all around me were nothing but noises I would expect from a mistreated dog.

There was a shrill ringing. A fire alarm? My whole body started panicking. The division head dug through her files and amid the mess she extricated – aha! – a phone.

I mumbled a "go ahead" to the slightly turned-away face to indicate that I wouldn't listen in on the conversation, but that I was still at her disposal, and drove home the point with a calm smile.

I glanced sidelong at her keyboard, biting back the urge

to hit a big fat Control-Z on this complete failure of a day in the making.

It was at that moment that I felt a warm breath on my calves; it couldn't be the computer fan. Since my interviewer's attention was elsewhere, I turned to peek under my seat but a sharp pain made me let out a cry. It was a German shepherd or a Czechoslovakian wolfdog or a bull terrier that had bitten my leg. It stared at me with one eye – the other was dead – as it panted, ready to bite again.

I was petrified, I dropped my head, and, very gently, pulled my legs up onto the seat, so that my knees were pressed to my chest, and then the division head hung up.

She looked at me, shocked. I shifted back into a proper position, praying that I wouldn't get attacked by the dog with its tail slapping the ground. The division head clearly didn't notice anything amiss.

Another groan – "kite disabled." I sensed that this was a question. What could I say? Tell her about being deaf, about my puzzlement, how could I explain all that without my voice shaking? The one moment I'd been fearing had come, she was now going to ask me a long string of awkward questions. Instinctively, to sidestep the matter, I replied:

"Disability in the workplace can be framed as a handicap. 'Handicap' is originally a horse-racing term that came about in the eighteenth century in England on the racetrack. The amount bet on one horse or another was placed in a single cap – 'hand in cap.' In France, it now means a race in which the competitors' odds are levelled by reapportioning the disadvantages."

And as she looked on, befuddled, I concluded: "So if you bet on me, you'll win the race by meeting your disability quota, so that's a win-win situation!"

She stood up, marking the end of our non-interview, offered me her limp hand, which I shook with my clammy hand, and directed me to the exit.

I left the prefab building with the strange hound dogging my steps. What could it be doing here? It tried to attack me, its teeth bared, but I stopped to tell it no, pointed my finger, and waited until all signs of hostility were gone. Nobody was looking twice at the dog, even though it was a sizeable beast with a black coat and a powerful body. I hoped it would disappear as fast as it had appeared, but it followed me all the way home.

In the building courtyard, I called my mother.

"Hi, Maman, it went fine. I still don't know what the position is, but I didn't ask, I knew I wouldn't understand the answer, the division head's voice ended up being one of those middle-register ones, I couldn't understand her. No!" I was yelling at the dog now.

"Everything okay?" My mother sounded worried.

"Sorry, a dog's been following me from the office."

"Call National Weather."

The National Weather Service? My mother always had the wildest ideas.

"Oh, hi!" I recognised my neighbour's voice. I pointed at my phone so he'd see I couldn't talk right then.

"Yes, Maman, I'll call the National Weather Service."

"No, no!" I heard my mother's stifled laugh, or maybe it was the sound of the connection cutting out because of the Métro. "Animal Welfare."

The neighbour gave me a sidelong glance as he took a drag on the cigarette pinched between his finger and thumb.

"I can't hear you, Maman, let's talk later."

But the god of dropped calls was a step ahead of me; the line was already dead.

I gave a cheek kiss to my neighbour and a kick to the dog zipping around us.

"I don't know what's going on, it's been following me around today," I said, nodding to the animal that seemed to want to play fetch.

My neighbour looked at me, befuddled, exhaling his smoke in my face. "Huh? What are you talking about?"

I looked down to see the animal had vanished. I brought my eyes back up to my neighbour's tanned face, feeling annoyed.

"Have a good day?" he asked, trying to play nice.

I gave him a rundown of my interview, or rather how it'd have gone in an ideal world. "Well, she'll call me soon to let me know, there are some other applicants." I had no idea if there were, but I wanted to say it.

"It's good that you were the first one she saw. Those jobs in French bureaucracy, you know, they get more applications than they know what to do with."

Lies can be a good thing. They give you some hope to cling to.

12

By some miracle, I got a call two weeks later. I guessed from the number on the screen that it was the government office, but my fear of phones had me paralysed. Transfixed by the blinking number, I couldn't pick up. I had absolutely no desire to find out whether I'd got the job or not. I had plenty of experience being in suspense; staying there a while longer wasn't hard at all.

My superego felt otherwise and I had to ask my friend Anna to listen to the voicemail they'd left me. The only part that sunk in was the important one: I was hired and I would start the following week. Now that was a downer.

Anna informed me that we were celebrating and that meant I was coming along to one of her weird little shindigs. "Just you wait," she promised me with a wink. Anna lived for evenings that spun out of control. Nothing made her happier than things going to pieces. "It's because I've got too much soul," she declared, even as a glint of sadness flickered in her eyes. I'd known her since we were little and poking dead things with branches. Back then, she'd thought my hearing aid was another tree branch, maybe that's how we'd ended up being friends. I did like the idea that a tree could be tucked into my ear, digging its roots deep into my auditory system and extending beyond the cartilaginous rim that was called a helix, straining towards the light.

I decided to play along and trailed her to the end of one of the RER lines. Anna's raspy voice combined with the train's noise in an overtone song. I was sure she was inundating me with those theories that sprang up in her head like mushrooms. The nice thing about Anna's theories was that she wasn't particularly attached to any of them. If I didn't feel like listening to them, she didn't mind.

A trip to Andalusia one August had acquainted me so well with Anna and her plump lips that I could now read them anywhere, anytime – even amid the fits and starts of lights along the RER.

The plastic earpiece of my hearing aid had cracked in a heatwave that August, so it was Anna's lips that gave me the lay of the land in the south of Spain. The crinkles and folds of her mouth enabled me to read all language's accents, and, in the pinch of her Cupid's bow, the different layers of irony. The sierras' rocky geography had been a monumental scale model of Anna's lips. Ever since, there'd been no need for me to hear her in order to understand her.

"Your ears are useless. They could just snuff it and you wouldn't care," she was saying. "Come to think of it, does this society really need to be heard?" Then she explained that at least it was a nice pretext to go full *Walden* and hole up in a cabin in the woods to the end of my days.

Whether or not I should consider Anna a voice of reason was something I'd always wondered.

On the RER that night, Anna's latest theory was from something she'd read, a quote that had stuck with her: "While we pursue the unattainable, we make the realisable impossible."

13

"One stop now," Anna said. I didn't even have time to glance at the RER map and pick out the town's name before we were already on the drizzly, icy platform. Only the streetlights offered any illumination in the dark night. A fogged-up Fiat Panda was waiting for us in the lot and we made a dash for it. We pressed our wet cheeks to the driver's bearded face, then the other passenger's clean-shaven one, before we climbed into the backseat. It stank like a dog, and I sat in quietly for the whole drive, obsessed by this smell and the memory it brought back of the one-eyed animal randomly appearing during the interview. Anna, meanwhile, was trading recollections in onomato-poeia with the two men.

The house where the party was being held was the pride and joy of those living there. They'd bought this drab place for a song and turned the premises into "living spaces". Insulation foam stuck out past the drywall like lichen and the linoleum squelched under the guests' muddy feet.

The host rang a little bell and then the clusters of friends were led to the dining room.

We were gathered around the oval walnut table in four pairs. Anna was beside me, making the introductions: Sébastien the bearded driver and Thomas the clean-shaven passenger had brought us here and now they were facing us. Then there was a retired couple: the woman, Émilie, had a face so pinched that I suspected that she had been dragged here by her partner and, as soon as there was a lull, she'd shoot him a triumphant look.

I think Anna had Émilie pegged as the guest who'd lose it first. Anna was always sussing out the weaklings, fantasising about playing therapist to a whole group of outcasts. Bookending us was the couple that owned the place – him a hunched-over stalk of asparagus and her a squat, plump piece of gnocchi. A gnocco? The conversation played out slowly, but I didn't hear the men's voices as they were too deep to reach my cilia. The candles jammed into wine bottles barely lit the faces and flickered at the slightest breath. A heavy laugh, a sigh from Émilie, or an exaggerated gesture would plunge us into near-darkness. And so I naturally ended up being the flame-bearer, making sure that the small fire was shared evenly among each of us. It looked like I came off as a Mother Teresa when I was actually a selfish pig. I'd lost all hope of keeping up; the only voices to cut through the tangle of sound were Émilie's and Gnocco's.

Once again, the host made a whole production of ringing the bell. "And now, dear friends, the first course!"

he announced exultantly before setting a china dish at the centre of the table.

At first sight, it seemed to be empty. The mouths around me fluttered with comments and laughter, then we all thrust our heads towards the centre of the table to see that there were small blue pills. Anna was delighted: *now* the party was really getting started. Everyone took one. "Wait!" Anna pulled out her tarot deck, and told us each to draw a card. She'd more than earned her nickname as "the card-teller".

My card was The Warrior.

We held up the small pills like communion hosts. I still wasn't sure what I was doing in this inaudible brotherhood. Gnocco leaned in to tell me about a spider that had once set up house in her ear canal – I had a knack for attracting all sorts of stories about ears. She was breathlessly describing all the sounds she'd been amazed to discover, the most surprising of which had been that of the spider spinning its web. I chimed in with what I knew about military research on their threads. And so, trading flecks and more flecks of spit, we wove a small cocoon of friendship and saliva.

14

A particular lightness overcame me: the heavy curtain of background noise was lifting.

Conversations spilled into one another. Other voices' words won out over Gnocco's speech. But I didn't know who was talking; the sounds stayed two-dimensional. All the sentences made up Exquisite Corpses of sound. I cosied up to the low voices, I stood in front of Sébastien, amazed by his timbre; I felt like I was in a bell that chimed with each of his consonants. My belly shivered with his *r*'s, as if I were the very mechanism that set the phoneme rolling in his mouth. Everything was so clear; I slipped into Sébastien's thoughts on stellar sound waves, Thomas had his own two cents to add. Nothing got past me, not even Émilie and Gnocco's discussions about jealousy.

The procedure had worked, I'd gotten my ear back, I was hearing even better than before!

I wanted to celebrate my regained ear with Anna, but she was gone. I heard the sound of my trainers squeaking on the ground, the scraping of chairs on the floor. A laugh began to rumble like a storm and ran through the crowd.

My ear was drawn to these steadfast sounds. I wanted to tumble through the laughter as if it were fresh grass, and I wanted Anna beside me.

"Hey, where's Anna?" I asked the giggling mouths. Nobody answered.

"Hey, where's Anna?" I asked, louder. Only eyes turned to me. I left the circle of mouths to prowl other rooms and find Anna. The laughter slowly grew less distinct. Was this also part of being able to hear? Experiencing the relief of a sound fading with each step further away?

I'd only ever heard in black-and-white, and now I was hearing the full range of sound within space. Then, at the end of the dark hallway, through a door that hadn't been shut all the way, I saw Anna's hair clinging to the light. Who could she be dancing with? Everyone was gathered in the big room. But Anna had never needed anyone.

I gently pushed the door open, enough to see Anna's outstretched arms whirling, her head thrown back, and enough to realise that she actually wasn't alone. She was twirling fast, so fast that all I could make out was the light tint of her hair and the blue clothes of the brown-haired dancer. I froze: Anna was dancing with my soldier. He had her spinning like a dervish, his body stiff in his be-draggled clothes, his greatcoat open to his gleaming torso, the beads of sweat as bright as the buttons of his over-coat. Everything about them glistened: Anna's curls, her teeth, the soldier's torso and his gilded buttons, it was like the morning dew had fallen on their sacred dance.

I watched them lose themselves in their round dance, which slowed little by little. Once they'd come back to earth, trembling and panting like dogs in the heat of summer, I drew close, a happy smile across my face. Anna's laugh softened slightly. I heard the air being drawn into and pushed out of her ribcage, I heard for the first time a small asthmatic whistle in her breath. As for the soldier, I picked out the smacking sound that his tongue made as it ran over his lips. Everything was so overwhelming, I couldn't get over it. I heard like I'd never heard before.

15

The soldier rolled a cigarette in his calloused hands and offered it to Anna, as if they'd been together forever. Anna dragged us both into a small alcove separated by some velvet drapes from the rest of the room. We sat on cushions under an old lamp with a tattered shade and shared the cigarette in silence, sneaking sly glances at each other. I relished my regained ear: the smoke that they inhaled made a warm sound, a waning whistle that ended on a high note. I heard my breath stretch out in pleasure; they answered with sensual sighs. The soldier's green eyes shone, his lashes batted suggestively, his eyes' whites were bloodshot, and his lips were slightly parted. Anna and I were enraptured by his mouth and his gaze rested every bit as intently on our own mouths. For a good while we simply took in the veins of his neck, our eyes following the last drop of sweat trickling down a treasure trail as the man scrutinised our faces, lingered on our jawlines and necklines. We looked at each other like souls that hadn't felt human warmth in ages, as if we were the last humans alive. Suddenly Anna burst out laughing, throwing her head back, then hummed a tune that the soldier seemed to pick up on.

In a low tone, she sang: "Do not forsake me, oh my darlin' / . . . I do not know what fate awaits me / . . . I'm not afraid of death but, oh / What shall I do if you leave me?"

Was it a song from some film? Anna liked to hum such things right when nobody was expecting it, and it always worked, there was always someone ready to hum along.

The soldier chimed in with his cracked voice, his eyes on me: "Do not forsake me, oh my darlin' / Although you're grievin', don't think of leavin' / Now that I need you by my side / Wait along, wait along / Wait along / Wait along, wait along / Wait along, wait along . . ."

I placed a kiss on the soldier's lips, swollen with grain alcohol or perhaps rubbing alcohol, feeling oddly as if I'd come up with these words. Seeing my baffled face, the soldier whispered: "Don't forget."

Actually, I wanted to forget everything and stay here forever.

They hummed the song again from the start, louder and louder, and Anna ran her hands through the soldier's hair, swaying back and forth.

"Anna, that's the man I was telling you about."

She nodded, then asked the soldier for a war story and he launched into a recollection of a card game in the trenches, an evening when one of the infantrymen had pulled out a photo of a woman instead of the Queen of

Hearts. "That picture of a lady drove me crazy." He hadn't been able to shake it ever since. He was besotted – or was he lovesick?

"Do we look like her?" Anna asked.

At which point the band made its loud entrance, with a frenzied Émilie leading the charge and Thomas and Sébastien right behind, and they were clearly all thinking about sex. Émilie let out a wild laugh as she shouted: "You heard me, anything you can do, I can do better!"

Anna glanced down the hallway to see that Émilie's partner was on his own, looking sad as he petted a dog. Then she winked at me, delighted by the turn the evening had taken, before joining the boisterous small group gathered around Émilie, who was undressing in this "living space", and I thought: now *that's* what I call living!

16

When I woke up, the soldier's scraggly hair was tickling my nostrils. I could smell Anna's warm breath as she, too, was curled up against his chest. The soldier's skin had always been pockmarked, but, as it was bloated from the night and the booze, it now felt smooth. Anna's mouth was mottled from kissing bodies and I was naked. To my right, Thomas was exhaling onto my neck and his hand was on my hip, I could feel his early-morning hardness against my bottom. I didn't see Sébastien or Émilie or Gnocco but I could make out their forms in the sheets on the floor. I'd taken out my hearing aid and I couldn't remember where I'd put it. Feeling worried, I extricated myself from the pile of bodies to go find it. I rummaged through the heap of clothes for something to put on, since my own were nowhere to be seen. I patted around all the evening's bodies, moving and otherwise, for my hearing aid, but I kept coming up short – until the soldier held it out to me. In his big hand, it looked like a sleeping seahorse. I turned it on and thanked him, but I didn't hear his answer.

People woke up and reached for their clothes, bent over like gleaners. I couldn't hear their footsteps and their voices anymore. Thomas kissed my cheek and whispered something I didn't understand. Sébastien gave me a conspiratorial wink: "Rather glimpse."

"Rather what?"

"Water clams," he repeated.

"Are you talking about clam diving?"

He burst out laughing and so did everyone else who was awake now, but I couldn't hear the laughs the way I had yesterday.

The soldier gave me a piece of paper before vanishing: "I told you not to forget."

"V-silk, all Tahitian. Stomatology is a unicorn matter."

It wasn't clear if Thomas was talking about Netflix, Tesla and Uber taking on a new industry. Or if he was talking about colon issues, or silkworm farming, V-necks, or things from Tahiti.

Everything was a muddle; the world was turning opaque again.

"Anna," I said, "the effects have worn off already!"

She was explaining that this was normal, that it wasn't supposed to last more than a night. I sank into a torpor on the way home, the dog slobbering all over my skirt.

17

The next morning was my first day at work, so I was dressed to the nines. I watched the street through the windows of the overground Métro on the way there.

How did people manage to just get things done? Cross the street, answer the phone?

I inhaled the humid autumn air deeply before walking through the annexe's front door and going to the division head's office. It played out as I'd imagined: limp hand – inaudible speech – growing unease – tour of the office and introduction to colleagues – arrival at my desk. I had a faint impression that it was something to do with birth certificates.

I had to help customers to register them and finalise such matters with various administrative bodies.

They gave me the morning to go through the software user guide and "get my bearings".

After some fruitless conversations with my four colleagues in Births, I finally came out with what was off about me.

I took the time to explain the facts: left ear completely

deaf; right ear with a hearing aid; lip-reading needed to fill in a holey language.

I saw a lightbulb go on for them. It was nothing short of poetic that I needed light to hear. That was, until they had to repeat what had already been said more than twice: all the poetic-ness went to pieces, and I went from poet to idiot.

At the same time, those colleagues struck me as a form-less mass of sound covered by identical brown trench coats.

And yet one of them managed to break through. Her name was Cathy, she had freckles and a serious look as if I'd entrusted her and her alone with a secret. I knew her name was Cathy because she'd made a point of her first name.

"There's two Cathys here." I didn't catch the rest, what detail she'd mentioned to make her Cathier than the other.

She made me think of those ponies with rainbow tails from my childhood whose manes I'd shaved off.

Anna would probably say that this woman had read up on "personal branding". Anna loved imagining what books were on people's nightstands, especially when it came to folks she'd never met. In fact, the less she knew about someone, the more spot on her guesses tended to be.

I had high hopes that, with a bit of training, Cathy+'s voice would be stamped in my brain as "quality product" and I'd hear it clearly enough that I wouldn't have to read her lips.

She told me that she understood. I assumed she meant my ears. Given her hand over her heart and her sympathetically pouting lips, I deduced that she was "moved". Her gaze softened, I could see her light brown eyes drift as if I were nothing more than a pane of frosted glass.

She told me that I could count on her.

I spent the rest of the day taming the other colleagues. Up close, they stood out from one another. The other Cathy had hair less blonde than Cathy+'s, eyes heavy with makeup in the same hue as the sea-green wallpaper in my speech therapist's office, and a smoker's voice. "La" was all I picked up of the tall colleague's first name. He had to be named Nicolas, not Charles. My ear hadn't registered any of the rolled sounds and the *a* had struck me as so clear and distinct that I suspected it had to be paired with an *l* rather than the *r* that cast a shadow over vowels. As for Jean-Luc, I did hear his first name. Often double first names were easier, even if I didn't always nail the second first name, but in this case the ending *c* was so loud that there was no mistaking this one-syllable word for, say, the "No" of Jean-No. I congratulated myself on snagging a job in birth certificates: my inner first-name lexicographer would be unstoppable. I wouldn't be terrified of making introductions anymore. I found Jean-Luc, who looked like a teen who hadn't aged a day, somewhat touching, but there was something about him that bothered me, like he was the sort to rat out his cellmates.

Anna was waiting for me right after work. She wanted to get a sense of the place and see what my colleagues were like. She had a little chuckle to herself, like an underhanded sister might on the first day back at school. "But Cathy+ is perfectly nice," I said unthinkingly, feeling obliged by her attempt at inclusiveness. "*Nice?*" Anna said. "Offices aren't offices without office politics. Don't let your guard down." I reminded her that she was hardly one to talk about offices. Her claim to fame, after all, was never having passed a job interview.

18

The next day, I came in early. The sooner I started my day, I reasoned, the sooner it'd end. I found my canteen card on my desk – Cathy+ had set it up. I stammered thanks when she and the rest of the team came through the double doors of the emergency exit and waved to me. I dove into the leaflets I was given about being a contract worker and the internal documents about such things as how the staff representative was elected. On the slate of candidates for the next election were people with Cathy+ and Jean-Luc's last names.

As I watched the line form on the other side of the counters that served as our work stations, I started panicking. All these mouths that would enunciate first names, last names, maybe questions. I'd never been professionally obligated to answer questions only asked out loud.

Cathy+ and her rounded teeth were encouraging as the first "customer" walked up – I'd been told in no uncertain terms by an email that I took to be instructions for civil servants that we were never to say "client" or "patient", no matter how much patience was required to help others to be administratively born. I didn't get a chance to wave hello before he'd already launched into his questions, or, rather, a single, unending question. The texture of his voice was that of a rusty swing going back and forth, some words went back down his throat with the sound of a crank pulley while others increased in volume to reach my ear. His nose tugged at the top of his mouth, distorting his lips and shifting the words' centre of gravity such that I was looking at his tongue at an unexpected angle. I was lost, but I mustered my courage and handed him the birth declaration form with the calm smile of someone who had seen it all. Somewhat taken aback, he stopped talking, filled it out carefully, and handed it back to me with some embarrassment, then he shrugged his shoulders and left, making way for the second customer. This one was a fifty-something woman, with an accent that tugged at the corners of her mouth with every vowel and chopped up the syllables by hammering down every consonant. Maybe because she was foreign-born, she wasn't pleased that I had her repeat her one request: to dig up her daughter's birth certificate. I told her which steps she needed to take and she left with a string of okays, like a riff that helped with memorising a route. As other customers followed, I mentally repeated the mantra of "feigning madness without going insane" from *The Art of War* every time I felt like I couldn't understand anymore, when the acoustic onrush turned into a muddy swamp and the lips' soundtrack stopped illuminating anything.

I also had to send acknowledgements of receipt, to confirm a new existence with various administrative bodies, heavy with the odd sensation of bureaucratically giving birth to new futures. It only took two words – a first name and a last name – and society would do the rest.

Then it was time for lunch. My memories of such meal breaks were rooted in childhood and boiled down to wet bread and ground beef launched across the room, nonsensical conversations started up by full mouths in the din. A din I came face to face with again upon walking through the canteen door.

Standing by the self-service line, I tried to see if there were other disabled workers. I'd read that French government offices tended to hire a hundred a year. I scanned eyes, ears, feet, arms for prostheses of one sort or another, then, not seeing anything, I looked for oddities and my gaze stopped on the belly of a woman who seemed to have been hollowed out by wartime shelling. But then I felt someone else's eyes on me, and I turned to see a colleague staring at my hair, and I stopped playing spot-the-disability and sat down at the end of the table, next to Cathy+. I could tell that the Cathier of the two was doing her best to include me in the circle of people hunched over their mashed potatoes and merguez sausage, felt the hand she had placed on my forearm, as if to keep me from vanishing, to stop my body from being like a chameleon and turning the colour of these mashed potatoes, and above all to show everyone else as well as me how much she mattered.

Jean-Luc seemed annoyed that I could act normal. I think he was fascinated by my hearing aid, but couldn't really make sense of my disability. He let out a whistle when I told him that I could follow a phone conversation by using a special device, but the next minute he was eyeing me suspiciously as if this disability had simply been a ruse to land this job.

I came back to my desk drained by the effort it had taken to follow the proto-conversation with my colleagues. Shortly after, I registered a floral trifecta: Rose, Hyacinthe, Camélia.

I was so exhausted by the lunch break that I could barely decipher the afternoon "customer" requests. Whenever I was too overwhelmed, I redirected customers with incomprehensible questions to Cathy+ who seemed to shift slightly, darkening, something in her eye hinting that I couldn't solve all my problems that way.

I took solace in the thought that I hadn't been born disabled, that I hadn't achieved disabledness, that I'd had disabledness, exactly like these customers, thrust upon me.

As I emerged from the building at the end of my day, the dog was waiting for me and followed me, barking at all the passers-by. By the time I got home, I was so distracted by the animal whose tail kept slapping my ankles that I ignored my neighbour and didn't answer my mother's call. Dog aside, I didn't have the strength to talk about my first days at work. All I wanted was to curl up in my soldier's arms. The dog joined us as if we were its masters.

"I'm not hearing any better, maybe it's even worse. The procedure didn't work," I told the soldier as I thought about the audiogram and the craggy landscape it had revealed. "Am I going to reach sea level at some point?"

To soothe myself, I said the word "sobriquet" over and over.

I liked pronouncing disused words, even if I didn't hear them without my hearing aid. By uttering them, by feeling them on my lips, I was making a pact with language.

19

That time passed was reassuring, but I was scared of getting buried in December and its long stretch of night. My colleagues' behaviour made no sense to me: Cathy+ seesawed between brightness and bitterness; Jean-Luc would relax in my presence every so often only to go back to being a control freak; as for "La" with his tuft of hair as stark as a cliff, our collegiality was expressed in a politeness so formal that it bordered on animosity. Cathy–, though, was truly fascinating. She had photos of puppies and babies pinned up at her counter. At a distance, all I saw was a jumble of soft fur, plump limbs, and the occasional glassy eye. Such love for everything newborn, such disinterest in what came after – landing a job at Births was clearly fate.

Suddenly, Cathy+'s voice broke through and, with it, all sorts of stories about her life. She had a teenaged daughter who took pride in turning every little thing into a huge saga that of course sucked in her beleaguered mother: a student get-together that devolved into alcohol poisoning and a stay at the Henri Mondor Hospital, a night at the police station, a domestic matter that involved firefighters. I couldn't help feeling jealous of this stage of life where people were still in a cartoon, where they could keep falling and picking themselves back up with stars spinning around their heads, but as I saw Cathy+ with her life at the beck and call of someone else's, bound permanently to it, she was the only one who came off looking heroic.

The days went by slowly. I tried not to feel bad about asking Cathy+ for help, even if I could sense her mood swings: one minute especially sweet with winks as rapid-fire as a submachine gun and fingers as gentle as octopus tentacles across shoulders, the next snappish, glaring down, pursing her lips, her hands retracted into her cardigan like hermit crabs into their shells. Sometimes she got up and told me to watch her counter for a few minutes, as if she wanted me to notice she was gone even though there were no customers and Jean-Luc was supposed to answer her phone.

One day she rushed off and I decided to follow her, counting on the hallway carpet to muffle my footsteps. She disappeared into a tiny room – a former toilet – that served as a break room with a rough-hewn door that never shut properly. Through the crack, I could see her sitting as she took a pill container out of her jacket, shook out a tablet, and swallowed it quickly, and then the door must have squeaked slightly and her eyes landed on mine. I saw what looked like a wave of fear run across her face.

She glanced around, clearly wanting nothing more than to disappear – I wished I hadn't followed her to begin with – and as she realised there was no way I hadn't seen everything, her shoulders slumped. I reassured her I wouldn't tell a soul. "Not a soul," I insisted. Secrets were what I knew best. She didn't care about my promise; she was staring at the floor and her lips explained to me: "You know, I'm told to apply myself to my work, but I'm still not a permanent employee."

"Permanent" was a word on everyone's lips in the staff canteen, it was easy to pick out the French word, *titularisé*, with its string of extreme vowels, the pile-up of *i, u, a, i, é* causing faces to shift as the adjective shaped both hopes and careers. My gaze bore into hers as I tried to convey all my support, but her eyes glowered; she was angry that I had caught her in her moment of weakness. I apologised, she straightened her back as if nothing had happened, and she became Cathy+ again, her face cheerful, her obliging expressions ready to be deployed in a snap. I stepped back to let her pass and she headed back to her station in a hurry, taunting me with her brisk pace and speeding through her work for the rest of the day.

I put even more energy into proving myself. I conquered my backlog of data entry and then double-checked it all for accuracy. I even offered to help each of my colleagues tackle their own backlog if they wanted, as my concentration skills were well above average. My faulty ears had primed me for exactly that. Cathy+ glanced at me, kicking her smile muscles into gear, but her grins were unseeing; I was no different from any of her customers.

I left work with this odd feeling that I wasn't able to make sense of reality anymore. I was following the roots of the chestnut trees cracking the pavement in the darkness when I heard a scraping or what I took to be an iron shovel along the ground. Then I caught a whiff of grain alcohol or rubbing alcohol, and only then did I see the form of my soldier, a hunched-over shadow.

"Are you there?" I called out.

He answered something like "I'm not so sure I am."

That bothered me and I thought out loud: "It'd be nice if language could stop being such a mystery." Then, since he shouldn't have to deal with my annoyance, I added: "Well, how are you, anyway?"

"How am I? I've been lying in a snowy, bloody field thirty days now, that's how I am."

20

The last two weeks of November were hard going. Night felt omnipresent on my commute to work and back home. The bus stop was on the broad boulevard and to get to it I had to follow my street all the way to a corner then turn onto the vast dark stretch of the artery road. At those moments I had the feeling of descending into a well. Each time, right at this crossing, I thought about how sound and sense rarely aligned: the French word for "night", *nuit*, has a light, sharp, radiant vowel, while *jour*, "day", has a dark vowel.

At work, the cold had frozen Cathy+'s voice. Her sentences were icebergs out of which only a handful of words emerged; her friendliness was mechanical. Sound and sense were out of joint. I still couldn't tame the line of customers. I only understood every fourth question; I sent every sixth customer to Cathy+ or Jean-Luc, taking advantage of my youngish appearance, which made me look like a somewhat inept trainee.

Between Christmas and New Year's, the holey sweater that Anna had knitted for me and the string lights I'd almost electrocuted myself with at my mother's, the government announced that it would reduce civil-servant numbers. And so, in January, a booklet with the forbidding title of *La ténosynovite de De Quervain* suddenly made its presence known among the staff. Cathy+ leafed through this "Guide to Diagnosing Musculoskeletal Injuries Attributable to Repetitive Strain" assiduously, asking management for ergonomic mousepads, but all we managed to get were pens with comfort grips. The election for staff representative was coming up, and the tension between Jean-Luc and Cathy+ was palpable, as they were members of different unions. As the job cuts loomed, rumours swirled. I didn't need ears to know what everyone was saying. And besides, the same words were on all their lips, first whispered then spoken openly. "Just a few little domestic thorns," Anna kept saying with a roll of her eyes as I gave her the rundown of my day.

21

Then came the announcement that the "restructuring" would happen sometime in January. My colleagues eyed me even more suspiciously. Maybe, knowing that I was a verified disabled worker, they figured that HR was going to keep me even though I'd only just been hired, that I was robbing them of their futures. What was I supposed to say to that?

I recalled what my speech therapist had told me: "You're not the only one. Deaf people are a tricky thing in the office. Some companies won't even hire them."

I'd never met any hard-of-hearing people; being in denial had cut me off from that lifeline.

"You've built a life as a hearing person, but you have all the same problems as any deaf person. That's not obvious to folks in general – they can't see that you're in a no-man's-land."

"I'd like to meet some others."

And so I waited for him to put me in touch with other hard-of-hearing people.

When I told Anna all of that, she asked: "What is it you're looking for?"

"A part of myself."

22

To ring in the new year, Anna had a small gathering at a bar with a few friends. I sat with them, had a drink. I was relieved to see Anna but worried about this group; there was already a woman trying to talk to me. I could tell by how she kept glancing at me. Just my luck that she had not only a middle-register voice – the timbre that had slipped into a black hole – but also serious problems pronouncing things correctly. I eventually gathered that she'd recently had surgery. She must have heard about my auditory misadventures from Anna. That was the only reason she was going to so much trouble to strike up a conversation with me, my attempts to extricate myself notwithstanding. We might have had similar experiences, but I didn't want to get into all that after such a rough day at the office, let alone run the mental obstacle course of trying to understand her – the only things I wanted were a beer, a laugh, and a nice time at a noisy bar where everyone present was as good as deaf. At some point, the conversations would be pure oohs and aahs of joy.

But Middle-Register-Voice-with-Pronunciation-Problems

clearly wasn't of the same opinion and while we were having a smoke outside, she seized the opportunity to sidle up to me and bury her head in my hair, hoping to find a receptive ear. I yanked back my head, forcing her to look at me straight on, and explained that I read lips, which she answered with a gesture to the braces on her teeth to make it clear that she wasn't keen on that. The dog knocked her glass of beer onto her skirt. "I'm sorry," I said. That was a total lie. I got a reprieve while she was putting things right: patting her skirt dry, getting a new beer.

This incident, along with my repeated insistence that I didn't understand a single damn word she was saying, only made her drone on even longer. I finally managed to figure out that she was giving me a rundown of all the hard-of-hearing people she knew, starting with her grandfather who had long refused to use any device that could help.

I imagined that she was telling me stories I already knew by heart: a grandmother complaining that the grandfather didn't understand a thing anymore, a family torn apart by the grandfather's denial and the mounting tension at family dinners.

I turned off my hearing aid, I got snippy, and I only answered her words with bored nods. She laughed. She had to be telling me about the time the grandfather had made a mistake and put his hearing aid in his dentures glass or, no, by the looks of her bursting out in laughter, the time the maid had found the hearing aid in the cat's dried vomit.

Anna and the others had gone back inside quite a while earlier, and all had understood from my evident signs of frustration that the conversation was going nowhere, but Middle-Register-Voice-with-Pronunciation-Problems seemed to be having a blast. When I started getting showered with flecks of spit, I blurted out that I really couldn't hear her and that she was going to all this trouble for nothing. That was my only way out at that point. Of course she took it personally.

(Anna burst out laughing and said: "Sometimes, Louise, you really can be a little shit.")

23

I was four months in and my soldier, hoping that I'd successfully got through the probation period, had been teaching the dog to bark whenever a cloud went by. He was convinced that this way I could be alert to changes in light and be prepared while reading lips. The only problem was that, this morning, once I got to the office, the dog was gone.

A small line had formed; I was the first staffer to arrive. I sat down at my work station as the customers filed in.

"Hello," I said to the first one.

"I'm here for the art, they said I should come clear for the certificates. And declare."

"Did you witness the birth?"

His answer escaped me. He seemed upset. I could see that the question seemed intrusive. Some people seemed shocked, others took it as an invitation to describe the whole experience, which meant they made themselves at home at the counter like they were at a bistro. Even without working ears, it was obvious this was boring for everyone but them.

I wanted to hand him the prefilled form for a birth declaration, but there weren't any left. There had been a whole ream on my desk yesterday, though. If there were no forms, the customers had to spell out everything so I could enter the data on the spot. I went to find some paper so they could write it all down, but every single form seemed to be gone, or moved. Was this my colleagues' doing? The work of Cathy+? Seeing the impatient line that had got even longer, I had no choice but to enter impossible names directly into the computer. Their round lips were like the street signs: red circles with their tongues serving as the red bar that meant *no, no, NO.* All I could hear were the dog's barks in between clouds.

I mangled a hundred first names and last names, I midwifed administrative monsters before the customers' furious glares: Frantz Soimit, Béné Lope-Vega.

When I saw my colleagues turn up at the end of the morning looking especially carefree, with Cathy+ at the helm, it was yet another slap to the face. My cheeks were red with shame, my body shaking with nerves. All the smiles, all the hellos, Cathy+'s "bon appétit" echoed and revived that slap.

24

Wrung out by the day, I headed to speech therapy, hoping for some comfort in the waiting room's sea-green hues. "You're drowning yourself in a glass of water," Anna had once told me about my attempts to deny being deaf.

No sooner had I entered the speech therapist's office than I said: "But why would I want to hide it at all costs, why has everyone been playing along?"

"Because everyone wants normality. You were hearing well enough to hide it and that was working. But now that you've moved from moderate hearing loss to severe hearing loss, you can't mask it anymore. Close your eyes and practise picking out male and female voices, children's voices, and so on, using only your ears. That'll force your brain to get better at picking up particular sounds amid the background noise. And make a note of the sounds to memorise them. Just try your hand at it."

Try my hand? Now that was ironic, considering that I was getting closer and closer to needing sign language.

25

Amid the background noise of the bus home, I tried to isolate the tires' screech, the engine's whine, the cars' honking, the voices, the shrill cries. I narrowed my focus on these irregular breaks, these gaps in meaning. The shrill barrages met thrumming. Hacking and slashing my way through, I cleared enough space around a rhythmic sound pattern that I deduced had to be a conversation between two people. Then my ear zeroed in on this particular subspace. The thrumming subsided and all that remained was the sharp staccato that alternated with throatier tonal ranges. I'd been told that high tones made it possible to catch consonants, that they gave words heft, propped them up like stakes that the vowels climbed up. The tone, the singsong rhythm led me to assume a woman's voice. Guessing the age was the second step. It wasn't a teen's voice; it struck me as too level. The thrumming started up again; a chimney pipe on a stormy night was clearly responding to this woman in her golden years. I was leaning towards short, two-syllable words punctuated with pauses. A small sharp cry escaped her mouth, the bus's wheels squealed, I turned to see them head off: a fifty-something woman accompanying an old, wizened man. My guess had been spot on. I could get to like this game. I'd learned how to dial my focus in and out, how to make myself at home in the city's soundscape.

Anna called me. I felt too cowardly to pick up; being alone was easier. I did play her rambling message where she was telling me that she'd noticed she was only dreaming of two-syllable words, that all the other words had disappeared. She felt like her soul was shrivelling up. I stopped listening. That image alone was enough to remind me of what I was losing, this feeling I couldn't shake that my ears were now a choke point for the soundtrack of my life. Yes, Anna, my soul felt like a shrivelled-up thing floating in formaldehyde.

I suddenly recalled Victor Hugo's words: "What matters deafness of the ear, when the mind hears? The one true deafness, the incurable deafness, is that of the mind." Some help he and Anna were!

That night, in the darkness of silence, the soldier and the dog were at the foot of the bed. Fear had me sitting bolt upright, staring at the horizon traced by our triad of eyes and mouths wide open in the night.

Only reading, only seeing the ink-black words intact in my hands, could assuage the dread of disappearing.

The sheets billowed up with the sunrise, hastening memories of the previous day, the forms that couldn't be found, the Paules or Sauls, the Basils or Patricks, all the first names I'd mangled and Cathy+'s triumphant grin. In the corner of the room, the soldier was chewing on paper. The dread of loss closed in on me again, swept aside only by the need to preserve, to archive the sounds I still had. Starting with the hail that I had heard in the flat's living room. I recorded it:

Home

Latin name: *grandō*

Vulgar name: hail

Latitude: 48.8355906

Longitude: 2.344926100000066

An avalanche of baby teeth.

The tenth of January. Summons day. The previous week's happenings had reached the ears of management and I had been called in to "clarify matters". That morning, on the way over, I'd taken note of the motorcycles' beastly thrum, a sander's whirring, the bass line of traffic jams that I mistook for the tide. As I went through the building's glass door, I felt the air shift, grow heavy, the sounds' vibrations become muffled. It felt like I was entering a damp grotto, like I was a hydrophone entering a submarine Everest nearly two full leagues below the ocean surface and hearing whale calls by the reception desk, boat motors as I walked past the copy room, and other mysterious sounds in the hallways: tectonic shifts, gasps, sighs.

There, one of those sighs. "Elo avazit." The HR director pointed to a chair in her office. I checked that she wasn't talking about a Scandinavian liquor and sat down, out of breath.

"We've been hearing about some murks and tides—" *cackling*.

A head poked into the doorway, and my interviewer

and the scalp traded some words that I, the deep-sea hydrophone, couldn't catch.

She immediately thrust out a contract that read "Job: digitisation. Level: 8. Division: death certificates".

Then I was led underground, making my way deeper into the building's bowels. I held my new contract as if it were my one obol to pay the ferryman taking me from one world to the next. In the weak light, the maze of concrete corridors resembled bleached coral. I accepted my lot in silence.

28

I had six months to digitise 783,954 death certificates, starting with the ones from 1914 because a hundred thousand soldiers' bodies were still lying in the battlefield. Every so often, bones accompanied by ID tags were exhumed and we had to officially recognise, a good century after the fact, that these men were dead. Some death certificates from the same time had escaped France's National Archives. I was dealing with papers that had the most surprising headings: "PARTIE À REMPLIR PAR LE CORPS" or even "EXTRAIT DES MINUTES DES ACTES DE DÉCÈS". I didn't see how corpses could be filling out paperwork or death certificate archives could have minutes.

Being underground suited me. I didn't have to deal with Cathy+ or the others anymore. I could skip the staff canteen and subsist on sandwiches and dust. I was less delighted, however, about restarting my probation clock in this new role.

I felt betrayed. Anna curtly pointed out that it was better to have been betrayed than to betray.

A man was talking to me. I raised my eyes to his lips. He was asking me for a death certificate that was less than three months old. But as his wife had died three years earlier, there was no document that was less than three months old. The distraught man explained that he couldn't remarry without this document. I called colleagues, to no avail. The man was shaking with fury. I wrote down his contact information and took him to the end of the hallway, scraping my skin along the walls as we walked. I let out a bark of pain, a Cerberus at the gates to hell.

I ended the day by recording one hundred F/A/45/879/E deaths without any food or break and then came back up to ground level.

At night it rained, so I took the opportunity to focus on footsteps, trying to gauge heel heights with my eyes shut. I made a basic chart to fill in:

<3cm heels		
3–5cm heels		
>5cm heels		

Having reached my neighbourhood, where every road had an aftertaste of home, where the streetlights reminded me of the nightstand lamp by my bed, I happened upon my neighbour. Even his breath smelled like worry: a mix of cooked endive and Pall Mall. "Are you sure you're all right?" he asked, and when I didn't react, he explained that

I'd been acting strange lately. He hadn't been able to resist keeping an eye on me – I didn't know he could see into my flat from his window – and had caught me talking to myself, pacing worrisomely, curling up on the sofa, leaving my lights on at all hours and, sometimes, setting off projectiles that exploded mid-air; it had got to the point that he'd wondered if he should call the firefighters.

What business was it of his? I left him mumbling, then scribbled down in my herbarium of sounds:

Home

Latin name: *siren siphonarius*

Vulgar name: fire truck siren

Latitude: 48.8355906

Longitude: 2.344926100000066

Overtone song of Red Sea snails.

29

My weekly get-togethers with Anna were critical. At the agreed-upon time, she opened the door wide, then held out her arms, into which I collapsed, playing up my exhaustion.

"You smell like old things," Anna said with a giggle.

Probably the smell of the basement, the same way that people who work with fish smell like the sea. I think it was more that I reeked of loneliness.

In the sitting room was Thomas. It was the first time I'd seen him since the party.

Anna winked at me, grabbed my hand to lead me in. Thomas gave me a kiss on each cheek. I didn't hear his voice as he did so, but the smell of his mouth, the coriander tinge of his breath, led me to believe that he had said something. I answered with a "hello", my throat tight with worry all of a sudden. I talked to fill up the space, so I wouldn't have to listen. I told him about how we were recording our lives ad infinitum through our connections to all sorts of institutions, from maternity wards to schools, hospitals, tax agencies. I talked about how urgent things were in the archives, paper crumbling from too much lignin, the material in wood that gradually turns it brown. My monologue wrapped up with the role archives played in conflicts, how Napoleon had seized those of the papacy, Hitler those of his enemies, Stalin those of the Nazis.

Thomas's lips parted. His face was freshly shaven, and yet I could see every black follicle beneath his skin. I hadn't noticed those playful dimples around his mouth before. My wariness was such that I didn't even hear him; my whole being had stiffened into a soundproofed case. To keep up appearances, I peered deep into his eyes, they were so odd. That was the only part of him that felt out of place: his huge grey eyes still held that murky hue of stormy nights from childhood. As Thomas's mouth remained open, I gauged his self-assurance. He seemed like he could handle anything that came his way. I tried to pinpoint what made him authentic. As his toned arms swept through the air, I noticed the slightest shift back, a hint of absence, as if, beneath his fleshly humanity, he was, perhaps, a bit of a bird. I thought I could get to like this manner he had of being so utterly normal and yet ready to just up and away.

I had never experienced such an ordinary moment, empty of questions. I found myself thinking that the light was perfect, the day was perfect, and we were in the middle of this perfection.

Then his mouth paused in a pucker – that was how a question mark appeared on some plump lips. Anna answered for me: no, I didn't work in the archives; I had a digitisation job in partnership with the National Archives, to "clear their backlog".

That was exactly it, Thomas's mouth had been cleared of all build-up, it was empty. His low middle-register timbre was a destitute bellows, his utterances sometimes going the wrong way and slipping back down his throat to exhale invisible words.

Anna stepped out to do something in the kitchen, leaving Thomas and me to tiptoe around each other. Anna must have explained things to him while I was away because he slowed down all his movements as if we were two astronauts in orbit. Our motions were frozen, even the batting of his lashes had slowed. The lashes in the middle were longer than the others, forming a peak, not unlike a bird's beak.

In this weightlessness, we became co-conspirators, calling up memories of that night of free love at the end of the RER line. An invisible thread made of remembered caresses drew our laughing eyes together. The thread sent us spinning towards desire, although we moved slowly, since Anna could come back any second now, and the thread slackened, the recollections were wound tight again, his grey eyes winking one last time like a cut to black hinting at a new scene.

Anna returned with a tray of cocktail sausages and told us about how living things were handled, or rather how it would be better if they weren't handled. The topic du jour had been brought to the table with the ketchup and the hors d'oeuvres: intensive farming. Anna was so fixated on the matter that I actually wondered if she wasn't secretly getting off to videos of free-range chickens.

I did appreciate that Anna was taking up all the sound space and I could keep things moving with a "no" or a "yes" or a "that's right", I even managed to pick out an "of course" in Thomas's voice. I also retained his intonations, his gently piercing voice. In the small, quiet room, the words bounced off the white cushions to reach my ears slowly but surely.

Trust was a channel, a waterway, through which Thomas's low-medium voice flowed. Sometimes he even took the time not to say anything, with his voice rising and falling, a vibrato not unlike a wind instrument.

I heard Anna's sweet, whimsical thoughts: "We should have gods for each thing again, it'd all make sense again, *ineluctably*." (Anna loved stressing adverbs, just as she loved adding explanatory asides with a *nota bene* or a *see also* that on her lips seemed more like brusque exclamations.)

When Anna offered me a cup of Japanese tea, brackish liquid with things floating on the top that looked like larvae, I pointed out that the tea was full of worms. She and Thomas didn't so much laugh as cackle: "No, that's puffed rice." They looked at me like I was a child as I played along with a silent giggle.

People often gave me that sort of tender look when my round eyes were trying to keep up with the ping-pong of a conversation. It was usually followed by a slightly worried glance around, seeking out an answer from the other speakers to the question: *Who is she?*

30

Who was I? Someone uprooted from language. When Anna was in her phase of throwing out *arrivederci* and *baci* and *tutto bene* left and right, showing off her love of Italy due to some vague connection to the country on her mother's side and some vague memories of Italian lessons – I mainly figured she was summoning up fantasies of a sun-drenched Italy, villages buckling under the summer heat, with distant cadences of mourners wailing at length – and she was telling me, her hand over her heart: "I miss Italian," I got the feeling that I could just as easily say in turn that I missed the French language.

I'd never experienced the comfort of hearing a familiar language's soft rumble within a crowd, the warmth of feeling at home amid strangers. On the street, in the hubbub, the French language struck me more as the murmuring of factory-farmed chickens. When I was young, I must have been a plucked chick, quivering among the other babies with mouths dribbling language like drool.

I didn't have any memory of that.

Well, I didn't have any memory of words, of intonations, before my hearing aid, meaning before I was five. Did the world before then simply not have any acoustic contours? As I thought on it, I realised that I didn't have any memories at all.

Had I needed sound to activate memories?

Anna told me that Thomas liked me: "You're like a sea bath for him." I didn't get it. I figured Thomas was flattered that I read *his* lips. I must have looked like one of the many photos of lemurs Anna had taken in Thoiry then pinned up on the wall so I could look on in horror as she went into raptures over them. I hated that wall at Anna's place, enough that I'd nicknamed it the Wall of Shame: the landscapes of Chamonix facing off against the calendar of naked French rugby players, black-and-white photo-booth strips, lines of gutter-punk lyrics and, here and there, snapshots of her grandmother from the seventies.

"He really does like you," Anna insisted.

I think she couldn't see how afraid I was.

"But what are you afraid of?"

"Of being seen in the state I'm in."

"Well, it'll do you good to be on seesaw."

"On seesaw," even Anna's voice was twisting, being swallowed up by this monstrous silence feeding off words.

"Of pulling someone else into my whole mess."

"Louise, stop it, this is a whole new stage in your life."

I was starting to get tired of people's comments. Who were they to tell me how I should or shouldn't take things?

I felt so angry that tears started coming, I sobbed in silence as Anna looked on, ashamed.

She held out a piece of paper on which she had written:

$$\begin{pmatrix} x_{1t} \\ \vdots \\ x_{nt} \end{pmatrix} = \begin{pmatrix} \mu_1 \\ \vdots \\ \mu_1 \end{pmatrix} + \sum_{i=1}^{p} \begin{pmatrix} \varphi_{11} & \cdots & \varphi_{1n} \\ \vdots & \ddots & \vdots \\ \varphi_{n1} & \cdots & \varphi_{nn} \end{pmatrix} \begin{pmatrix} x_{1,t-k} \\ \vdots \\ x_{n,t-k} \end{pmatrix} + \begin{pmatrix} \varepsilon_{1t} \\ \vdots \\ \varepsilon_{nt} \end{pmatrix}$$

$$\rightarrow X_{t+h} = m + \sum_{k=0}^{\infty} C_k \varepsilon_{t+h-k}$$

I looked at it, not understanding.

She continued her mathematical proof on a new sheet and explained as she went:

$$L_t = L_{t-1} + \varepsilon_t$$

$$L_t = \sum_{i=0}^{t} \varepsilon_t + L_0$$

$$\frac{\partial L_t}{\partial \varepsilon_t} = \frac{\partial L_t}{\partial \varepsilon_0}$$

"Look, L is you, Louise, and t is time." Her voluptuous tongue stuck out between her teeth. Was Anna lisping? "So the Louise of today is equal to the Louise of time minus one, meaning yesterday plus the total time you've lived since" – Anna looked at me intently, to check that I was keeping up with the breadth of her knowledge – "which means" – Anna's pointer finger was on the second line of the equation – "that you're the sum of everything that's happened to you since you were born. This random walk is a non-stationary stochastic process."

"So, Anna, why should I care about this non-stationary masochistic process?"

For all her wisdom, Anna still didn't get my question. She locked eyes with me again, her lashes wide and quivering. Probably to make sure I'd get lost in the vast ocean of her knowledge.

"Listen. This shows that the effect of what happened to you long ago is the same as the effect of what happened yesterday. Each event has an equal effect. And you are everything that's affected your life."

"Okay . . ."

"Every single thing that happened while you were a hearing person is exactly as important as losing your hearing has been. The being 'Louise' is every bit as much who you were before losing your hearing as who you are now. Nothing has changed about 'Louise.' You are no less yourself than you were before. If you lose something, you haven't had anything subtracted from your being. Meaning: Thomas is lucky to meet you now."

She looked at me, proud of herself, proud of being

the learned friend and the friend ready to buoy my spirits however she could. She'd managed to get a small smile out of me.

One nice thing about Anna's theory, all the same, was that it shone a light on my weariness, cut through it to show me a way to an elsewhere.

32

Thomas's job title was "mobility consultant". I hadn't really picked up what that meant but what had stuck with me was that the byword of his field was "terrain". The way he saw it, we belonged to a ball of earth that was on the outskirts of the cosmos and our planet was a web of networks and connections, and he made sure things moved smoothly.

Apart from this watchword, I didn't remember much.

Whenever I observed him moving through a crowd, I felt like I was getting a glimpse of who I might have been if I weren't who I was, or who I might be if a cochlear implant allowed me to become normal.

I saw him:

– turn his head at the same time as everyone else to where something had happened;

– look up when a plane zipped across the sky;

– listen to conversations on public transit;

– respond quickly to various things said on the street, a polite smile on his face.

I felt like I could hide behind him, like he could erase all my clumsiness.

Watching him made living feel like something innate. This naturalness was something I felt on a physical level for the first time. (Later on, I tried to put words to this small thing he was giving me: like the moment of slipperiness felt in falling asleep and forgotten upon waking. He grimaced and said: "You should be feeling the exact opposite.")

But when he talked to me about mobility, did he realise how immobile I was?

When he talked to me about terrain, did he realise how up in the air I was?

When he said: "Do you like treed camels?" and I said: "What?" and he said: "Do you like greedsome elks?" and I repeated: "What?" and he said: "Do you like creeked-up pelts?" – did he realise how badly I wished I had an explosive belt because all of a sudden blowing myself to pieces in front of him really didn't seem like the worst idea ever?

33

In the speech therapist's waiting room, magazines with garish covers faced off on the table: *For the Deaf*, *All Ears*, *Hearing Research*, *Silence & Sound*, the most heavily leafed-through ones standing strong at the centre of the waiting room's side table. I picked up *Hearing Research*, at the top of the pile, a scientific journal that seemed to have articles about tinnitus and genetic disorders that resulted in sudden loss of hearing. It also had some touching accounts of teenagers and older people who urged readers to choose their treatment carefully and not to be afraid to seek support.

I quickly set it aside and picked up the magazine that was, sure enough, *For the Deaf*, but as I dug in I felt eyes on me. When I looked up, I saw a thirty-something sitting across from me on the other side of *Silence & Sound* – I hadn't heard him arrive. He looked away immediately. I observed him: Did he have an implant? A hearing aid? One or two? His mass of blond curls ensured that nothing was visible. I squinted to activate my zoom, hoping for some movement on his part but he stayed stock-still, his eyes fixed on the ground between his feet, then it was his turn to look up as I dropped my gaze and busied myself with "Deaf Agriculture Festival at the Filletières Goat Farm" while staying alert to what I could sense: the heat of his stare on my carefully combed hair.

Footsteps entered my field of view. I stood up and said "hello" to a slim, hunched-over young mother whose arms held a baby with an implant. The blond man didn't wave, he kept on staring at the ground between his feet. I sensed his curiosity about me evaporate. All the tension was gone, and he didn't look up again, as if he'd found what he was looking for. He must have figured out where I fell on the deafness scale. I wanted to strike up a conversation with him but he ignored me, until the speech therapist opened the door. A sudden breeze ruffled everyone's hair and I saw a glimmer. Maybe the cord of his hearing aid? When the doctor waved to him, he didn't respond, simply smiled embarrassedly, his cheeks reddening, then got up as briskly as an insect and gave me a sidelong glance before the door closed on his curly hair full of secrets.

I stayed put, settling into my unease, I'd sensed in the man the same shyness and the same avoidant gestures that I sometimes had with hearing people, and I realised that this visible discomfort was something I could provoke in other hard-of-hearing people. So I was less deaf than him – had he heard it in my voice? I was looking for someone like me, we all were, but it wasn't him and it wasn't me.

The newborn's implant seemed too big for such a frail ear and the drain plug jammed in the skull protruded from the peach-fuzz layer of downy hair. This baby's fate was playing out there: a life shaped in part with this implant, nothing like me, nothing like that man. This baby would grow up to be someone with an implant, a boy whose trajectory would be the opposite of mine: he was entering sound right as I was entering silence.

34

On the way to work, my dog's leash dug into my hands, yanking me away from the office, maybe towards the vast fields of rapeseed and corn and grain and sugar beet along Route nationale 4, which ran east beyond the Périphérique. The barking drowned out the motors, and I narrowly avoided getting run over twice. The soldier relit his cigarette compulsively, monitoring the city, shamelessly ogling the asses of passers-by in tight jeans, stopping to peer in the windows of vape shops with names like Smoke Me Up or Monsieur Vape-eur.

It was practically a battle with them to get to work on time; at the intersection, halfway to my job, in the morning rush, a sign caught my eye: NILS OYAT, HETEROGENESIS EXPERT, CONSULTS BY APPOINTMENT.

I took a photo to send to Anna and then returned to fighting to get to the office. I got there right on the dot, dripping with sweat, after losing ten minutes waiting for the soldier to pass through the security barrier at the entrance, getting rid of all his old "dumdum" bullets, those unspeakably cruel pieces of ammunition that burst apart within the enemy's wounds. He carried them around like holy relics. Insomnia had given the security guard, Sham, bloodshot eyes through which I was sure he saw a totally different world. He always seemed unperturbed, as if lost in his memories, and he let the soldier through, not even glancing down at the dog that nearly peed on the notice board.

We made our way below ground to the lair of the death-certificate archives. A brew of metallic and dusty odours embalmed the room and seemed to bring a heartfelt smile of reassurance to the soldier's face while the dog raced through the aisles. I settled at my desk under the fluorescent lights and returned to my mission of archiving the dead of the Great War. The soldier helped me sort the records by date and by the end of the morning we were a well-oiled machine.

I was so absorbed that I didn't notice the soldier's trembling hands and his misty eyes. After lunch, the papers he handed me were warping with his tears: "the death of", "the declaration of", "the death of Armand Amant". (The man's name was visible on the death certificate.)

He caught his breath, his curls shaking with his quivering heart, and added: "He told me about Venus, which he said couldn't ever be seen from Earth. He was a short fellow with red hair and all sorts of bizarre obsessions: he spent his days asleep and woke up in the evening to go up and down the trenches."

At which point the soldier showed me his shoes:

"I prised out all the nails, I had to use them for his name, on his grave. That's why nobody hears me."

Then he pulled a paper out of his pocket with a dried fern pasted on it. The date and place were noted next to it. "It's a wartime herbarium," he said.

Poppies, daisies, ivy, all bearing witness to his long march towards Verdun, Argonne, Champagne.

Our conversation had to end there. A colleague from the National Archives had arrived to see what progress I was making and had checked several of the digitised certificates to make sure that procedures had been followed correctly, that no steps had been skipped. As he went through onscreen menus, he clarified in a voice as rough and fragile as the documents I'd been handling, " . . . thousand linear kilometres of paper . . . hard to digitise things that have been all over the place . . ." A tug-of-war between my internal lexicographer and my memory of phonemes broke out, causing me to lose track of details, but I managed to catch something like "quality control".

Everything was in order, apart from my forgetting to check the "enable user verification" box at the end of the process for each document. He launched into a long explanation with each word trailed by that rumbling sound typical of people trying to figure out how to phrase things while keeping the listener in their vocal clutches, meaning that I had to exert myself even further to distinguish between words and continuous noise. All my attention was on picking apart what he was telling me, then I realised: the "enable user verification" option had to be checked *while* I was saving the digitised death certificate. This let the system make sure users weren't robots by having them identify where they saw dead people in a photograph from the archives.

My gaze took in all the movements, from those of the lips of the man checking over procedures to those of his fingers on the keyboard. As my eyes darted around, all I retained was a succession of *aaa*'s, the National Archives colleague's right-angled eyebrows standing in for consonants. I pieced together that he was asking me if everything was good. I whispered yes. He seemed more or less satisfied by this and eventually gathered his belongings, his coat and his briefcase.

35

It had been a month since our second meeting when Thomas, who was having drinks at my place with Anna, noticed one of my audiograms lying around in the entryway.

I forgot about that soon enough, but one April evening, as we were starting to officially "see each other", he dragged me into a dimly lit spot. "I don't like surprises," I said. He answered with a winning string of sounds meant to urge me to take the final step. "I hate dark bars," I protested. He took my hand and led me down the staircase to the cellar, an empty vaulted room. Lights amid the stones revealed the walls' dampness. At the back was a mixing console.

A perfectly clear sound cut through the air, and an electric-guitar note hung for a long while, round and full, a warm sound that made my throat quiver. Then, nothing, the sound reverberating in the silence, deep. And then it happened again, several more times. A low vibration in my throat, my skull enclosed in the electric membrane of sound – silence that held the preceding note in my memory – the leading note detonating, always the same one, expected, hoped for – velvety silence – smile on Thomas's face – expectant silence.

Then the saxophone unfurled in the basement, filled the space between my lungs, the crescendo of high notes filled me to brimming. Emotions poured through me like a river. I heard the charge, the breath that reached the instrument's mouthpiece. The dotted note that stepped back, the better to charge more shrilly, making my teary heart shiver, soothing my scorching-hot ears. A landscape of sharpened peaks crossed the blazing night and combined in my mind with the black-and-white images of night-time Paris, tinged by sound. (How could Thomas have guessed that *Elevator to the Gallows* was my favourite movie?)

Sometimes, not being able to hear well made me hypermnesic. In the clear, powerful final solo, which I'd never heard before, I could recall Thomas's lips translating the lines of a film: "Oh, personal life, sure. But it's so clumsy. Films are more graceful than real life" – at that I remembered the sight of Jeanne Moreau's beautiful self waiting in the café, in black and white, the fear so gentle, I remembered how both this fear and this waiting appeared so thoroughly polished, how this weariness seemed to have become beautiful through her pencil skirt and crossed legs – "Fims don't have traffic jams, they don't have useless down time. Films move along like trains, after all. Like trains in the night."

I did love *Blue Train*.

Later on, I recognised the first notes of the first bit of the soundtrack, which ran through me like they never had before.

I told Thomas that the saxophone was what came nearest to a human voice, and that I sometimes couldn't tell them apart.

Then he wrote down this Miles Davis line for me: "The real music is the silence and all the notes are only framing this silence," encouraging me to accept that silence came before sound.

At the end, I must have cried in happiness as the bass broke through, then the piano. I heard each instrument distinctly.

How was this possible? "Remember that audiogram?" Thomas had brought it to one of his sound-engineer friends and he had adapted *Blue Train* to my range of hearing, adjusting each frequency so it could best reach me.

36

When Thomas uttered the word *amour* for the first time, I didn't hear him.

Lips puckered / corners of mouth open wide, tip of Thomas's tongue between his teeth / lips half-open / slight inhale, lips quickly closed / eyes beaming.

"I love you" was a set of words I only saw spoken by stepfamilies living in big houses in American suburbs in B-movies. *Je t'aime* appeared in yellow subtitles and of course that made those words seem like pure kitsch.

Thomas believed in those words, as if they could unlock a secret passageway, while for me they shut doors. Then his lips crashed against mine, leaving me with the feeling that "*je t'aime*" was a code name for this accident.

I had fallen into Thomas, into this softness described by his body. I needed a garden stake. I coiled around him at night and let his breath instil me with a movement that I hoped was upwards.

I think, more than anything, I was reassured by the prospect of someone being in my life, as if what was useful about his presence was that it occupied the question of love rather than answering it.

Clearly that was the best thing I could do. Watching him love me was perhaps a way for me to come to terms with society.

37

After the concert that had sealed the deal with Thomas, I was stuck on the bus. A truck was blocking the road; it looked like a complicated manoeuvre between the construction site's gates and the sidewalks that were teeming all around, scooters and bikes slipping through the smallest gaps. The people on the bus seemed worried, annoyed, constantly glancing at what was going on, talking about it, nodding or shaking their heads, using their hands to show how they thought things should be done: reverse, go one way, go the other way. The hubbub got louder. The smell of exhaust alerted me to a motorcycle nearby, the heady scent of hairspray to a permed head walking past, the bitterness of sweat that a citrusy spray tried to drown out: smells opened up the space that had been sealed off by hearing.

We were still stuck as night fell completely and the city's lights made the landscape new again.

As soon as I turned off my hearing aid to escape the aggressive soundscape, everything became softer and all-encompassing, I took in a display of blinking lights:

headlights, traffic lights. Smartphone screens, too: night-lights relit by swiping fingers. In this muted space, the smells grew agreeable, like those of a long-sought trip. I smiled in bliss until my device, which I hadn't turned off properly, suddenly clicked back on, shoving me violently back into a bone-crushing city, shrieking in constant alarm. I rushed towards the closing doors, clearing a way through the compact mass of travellers, then, once outside, I hurtled into an alleyway so I could turn the device back off like I'd wanted, guided now by the streetlights and the fullness of silence.

38

Rather than spring air, I inhaled an odour of wet dog and exhaled it between my monotonous digitisations: remove staples if any – paper in machine to flatten it – scan settings – position sheet – press button – FLASH – FLASH – stinging eyes, burning eyes – check image quality – save file – share.

And, when I looked up, I could feel the silence, which wasn't really silence. I heard, rather, the sum total of all sound's absence. Silence was a muffling, as if the sounds were waiting just behind the walls. They were what heard me – my heart as it beat, my breath, my joints – and I heard them listening behind the thick walls of the archives.

I had the odd sensation of being observed by the sounds, these huge absences. But maybe I was confusing those sounds with the Great War dead whose existence was a matter of the papers filed on shelves. Like the dead, things were coming alive. I could feel their weight against my skin. I was surrounded by the noise of the dead, the silence of the living, the living-dead noise.

39

I left work wanting nothing more than to curl up somewhere nobody would find me. My day had been gloomy enough; the National Museum of Natural History and its gallery of comparative anatomy felt like a perfect hideaway and refuge. At the front, a horde of the biggest land mammals' skeletons cantered in the wind, their reconstructed frames giving the illusion of movement. The gallery of comparative anatomy made me think of a civilisation on the brink of disappearance, and that image struck me as akin to my own ears taking in what my brain saw as the skeletons of sounds. A tiny label informed me that Steller's sea cow had, in fact, been hunted to death and was thus wholly extinct.

I turned to the vitrines along the walls and was immediately snapped up by the tiny bell jars of mouse skulls against a midnight-blue backdrop, utterly fascinated by the interplay of shadow and light in these secluded cavities.

Absorbed as I was, I'd forgotten the growls. The dog was panting in front of the *Canis azarae* from Peru and let out a few sharp barks of fear.

Along the back wall was the teratology vitrine. In it monsters could be seen floating in jars of formaldehyde: a pig with one eye, a dog with a cleft lip, a carp with no head, two conjoined lambs. Teratology, the exhibit label said, is the study of malformations resulting from developmental abnormalities. These result from delayed or incomplete embryonic division or from genetic changes, whether inherited (chromosomal anomalies) or accidental (exposure to toxic elements, radiation, or infectious agents).

What about me? What kind of monster was I? I imagined myself frozen for eternity in formaldehyde, my nose wrinkled, my ear pricked up, my mouth open to utter my characteristic "what?" in such a vitrine. But it was hard to be sure whether or not I was a real monster: I'd never had genetic testing done, after all, and no other member of my family had gone deaf.

I shooed away the thought and kept on reading.

"Before the nineteenth century, these anomalies were presumed to be due to chance" – why else would this have happened to me? – "or the will of gods or the devil. They sparked the imagination: monsters of antiquity such as the Sirens, Cerberus, and the Cyclops in Homer's *Odyssey*; monsters inhabiting Hell in medieval works of art such as the triptychs of Hieronymus Bosch or Doom paintings on the western walls of churches."

The collective imagination had left deaf people on the sidelines; there was no Golden Legend around ruined ears. The deaf had no place in the founding myths of mankind. Man's empathy was inarguably reserved for the blind. In China, the deaf were cast into the sea; in Ancient Gaul, they were sacrificed to their gods; in Sparta, they were hurled off cliffs; in Athens and Rome, they were paraded in public spaces or abandoned in the wild.

Oedipus gouged out his eyes, but why? He ought to have punctured his eardrums instead. Going by the facts, his ears were the problem. Oedipus heard the oracle's message wrong, he was hard of hearing, he misheard the warnings. But deafness doesn't have the grandeur of blindness, let alone the stoicism. And psychoanalysis's infatuation endured through this mishearing. No, it really doesn't make any sense, psychologists aren't eyes or mouths, they're ears.

The final wall leading visitors towards the exit showed different organs that I attributed to sound: first were lungs, the organs of breathing; then hearts in every shape and size. Their function was to pump what made us alive; they allowed us to keep going.

The tongues of llamas, of hyenas – bad tongues – licked their nooks. ("Well, can't you hear when I say *th*?" my English teacher asked, emphasising the tip of the tongue stuck between her teeth. "Well, can't you hear rolled *r*'s? It's not that complicated," my Spanish teacher asked, showing me the back of her tongue in her wide-open mouth.)

In the next vitrine, grey squares with little black holes in the centre were nailed to numbered plaques. I looked at the label and read that they were fish ears. I pressed the button next to it, releasing a barrage of vibrations that reached my forearm. An illuminated panel had been hung to furnish further information: the sensory experience demonstrated how fish experienced sound: through vibrations.

The next square was wholly translucent: a jellyfish's way of hearing, the opposite of the black hole that, for fish and men, served as ear.

Instead of pressing a button, I could stick my fingers into a slimy mass that every so often clenched like a vagina. The little illuminated label explained that jellyfish have no ears, that they possess organs oriented towards the senses of sight and balance. I felt like a jellyfish, floating amid so much with no visibility.

An oyster served as transition to the human ear. I could stick my fingers into a different hole that pinched me. The illuminated label explained that oysters responded to hearing tests performed by a research team by snapping shut, especially at lower frequencies. Their sensitivity to sound vibrations allows them to hear backwash, sea bream, and ships.

The display ended with an explanation that those three things are detrimental to oysters by forcing them to open and shut far too often.

I could relate.

The vitrine devoted to the human ear was far less explicit than those of fish, cnidarians, and bivalves: it was a display featuring components of the human inner ear, small shards of bone, debris. They looked like splinters from wrecked boats eroded by salt and washed up with the tide on this display vitrine's shelf.

My ears had never been able to put to sea and drift towards other languages. I was, at best, a hybrid mixture of jellyfish, fish, and oyster.

40

Outside, everything seemed muffled. By next spring, would the world be blanketed in an even deeper silence? In my glumness, I hadn't noticed that I'd been getting closer and closer to the herbarium building of the National Museum of Natural History.

The building was exactly like the one for the gallery of comparative anatomy, apart from the path visitors had to take through the displays. They had to look down like mourners at the dried flowers under glass. The solid wood furnishings on which the herbaria were displayed looked like butcher's blocks with slim drawers that could be pulled out like chopping boards.

In the first display, I happened upon samples of wood from Easter Island. These little black strips lay in their dark frames as if in coffins. They were the sole witnesses to the island's long-vanished forest. Further off, dried flowers filled the displays with their curlicues. I felt moved as I traced their curves with my finger. I stopped for a while at the dried poppy, its petal almost transparent on the page. Did some sounds fade before they died?

I wrote down:

Jardin des plantes
Latin name: *folium mortem*
Vulgar name: dead leaves
Latitude: 48.84230
Longitude: 2.35953
Jawbone chewing dried flies.

But all of a sudden, I heard hammer blows. Like a construction site, but less mechanical. To distract myself, after I tucked away my sound herbarium, I slid my finger over the glass to remember the shape of the dried poppy. But the noise got louder. It was no use looking all around, focusing on the poppy, running my finger across my knuckles to remember how many days there were in March: the sound didn't change. It seemed like it might be footsteps, several heavy ones. But I was alone in the gallery. The hammering got so loud that I (foolishly) put my hands over my ears and shut my eyes. The poppy's shape lingered on my retina, dancing on the undersides of my eyelids. I imagined myself in a field of poppies: as the poppies proliferated, so the sound subsided.

But it was hard for me to keep that picture in my head and be rid of the hellish sound for good. I opened my eyes and everything was gone as quickly as it had come. In my confusion, I'd taken a few steps forwards and now I was in front of an enamel display label that read:

The poppy is a segetal plant, meaning that it grows in fields of grain. These flowers spread everywhere that trenches and channels are dug, but especially amid the chaos sown by the "storm of steel" that tilled hundreds of cubic meters and brought the limestone layer to the surface, mixing soil and flesh to form a perfect catalyst for millions of petals to unfurl and redden the battlefields of the Great War.

Suddenly I saw, in the corner of the room, not the museum guard but the soldier with his head buried in his hands. He was wracked by sobbing. Before I managed to reach him, a woman who'd popped up out of nowhere was offering him a handkerchief. I stood back to watch these two souls unaware of my presence. She was talking to him quietly and he kept glancing at her hesitantly. He took off his kepi and turned this way and that – I felt a pang of jealousy. The soldier's brown curls tumbled over his forehead. The night of sex came back to mind, my hands in his thick hair, the curls coiling around my fingers as his hand ran up my thigh. My unease grew: Which man was swimming back and forth in the aquarium of the night, the friend or the soldier? I couldn't stand it anymore: my jealousy began to bark, and the woman and the soldier startled but it was she who rushed over, looking panicked.

I turned around, hoping to see the dog turn up, but it

wasn't there. I was left with the thought that I and I alone had let out that animal cry.

"Are you all right?" The woman's diction was perfect, her lips took care to articulate each individual syllable. She was so close that I could see her thin, slightly creased skin with its liver spots and its two-ply-toilet-paper texture. When she realised I was inspecting her, she stepped back.

"I really do like herbariums," I said, to distract us from the awkwardness.

I rushed out so I could take refuge at Thomas's and coil like vines around his presence. In his flat, bodies and things all had their place, an orderliness that I could rest my eyes on, let my thoughts settle on. Here, my soldier and the woman had no hold on me.

41

Thomas dropped me off at work the next day. I went underground, and at lunchtime I had to return to the ground level of existence, leave the crackling and the fluorescent lights of the death certificate archives. As I had no interest in bumping into my old colleagues or going back to the staff canteen, I only went upstairs when nobody was around.

I usually sat in one of the blue plastic chairs by the fake banana tree. Except another human was already settled in there. I returned her hello, although I wondered if maybe it was a curse – like me, she couldn't have been too happy to see someone else. I didn't recognise her at all; her angular face was unreadable but she had an intriguing unflappability. I told her that I was deaf. With each of us under a banana tree leaf, our chewing stood in for conversation.

From that point on, Mathilde was my one ally. I borrowed her stick-insect technique to get close to her colleagues in the print room and shield myself from the ones in Births.

The car is matte tick / charismatic
What could he be talking about?
I looked back at the colleague from the print room:
"Pinnace
(the soldier scribbled "business" on a sheet)
isn't good. There cooked
("could", wrote the soldier)
be a reed organisation."
("That's okay, I've got it," I told the soldier. He still scribbled: "reorganisation".)

"Cortical reorganisation, or neuroplasticity, is what that's called. When someone can't make use of a particular sense anymore, the cortex reorganises so that area of the brain is repurposed by the senses that the person still has."

To save face in awkward situations, I was now in the habit of reading the *Anarchist Neuroscience Review*, a magazine my mother had given me a subscription to. She had to be thinking that I'd take on a more "revolutionary" stance towards loss and be more at peace with technology.

At heart, she wasn't wrong, I had to get used to the idea that one day I might get a cochlear implant. And that day would come soon enough. But when I read about other people's feelings of fear and fascination, the science of it all struck me more as a hardcore version of those trashy magazines I saw at the grocery-store checkout: "In a study of kittens deprived of vision by lid suturing or binocular enucleation, the distribution of callosal connections in the visual cortex was considerably sparser compared to normal adult cats."

I imagined my ears sutured shut or the cochlea bursting like a piece of popcorn, electrodes scattering across my forehead.

But one article I'd come across stopped me in my tracks: "According to these studies, deaf people show an increase in their ability to process visual movement. For instance, they are faster and better at perceiving the direction of movement in their peripheral visual fields and they produce higher-amplitude waves when visual evoked potentials are tested."

Faster and better at perceiving the direction of movement in their peripheral visual fields.

I had indeed noticed that my visual abilities were heightened. Even in the last rays of sunlight lips weren't wholly obscured; labial consonants persisted well into dusk. I could actually read out of the corner of my eye what the soldier was scribbling to avoid misunderstandings. He used every trick he could. There were times when he saved my skin with a text, and others when he just left me in the lurch.

42

The speech therapist was doing his best to verbally assault me. Inside the glass shell the small black speaker aimed at me was spitting out his lists of words and lists of sentences that I had to isolate from a backdrop of noise. I repeated in terror like a lab animal: "I only have one love" – his warm, ringing voice said "yes" and I kept going – "my first love is a wolf." I wasn't sure about that, I thought it might be "my first love has a roof." My speech therapist's cheeks swelled with a smile to help direct my memory to the right answer. And with that I was lost in hypotheses that got me further away from what I remembered of the sounds, the same way that describing a dream pulls the recounter away from its images. The first love here was a wolf – even if that didn't make any sense, that was the right answer. I was happy, because understanding "my first love is a wolf" distanced me from my animal condition.

Several knocks interrupted the end of the appointment. My speech therapist's glance towards the door made it clear that this was a real-life happening. A beanpole came in, and I narrowed my eyes at him, full of disdain at his impatience. Couldn't he just wait like everyone else? The same way I'd waited in the sea-green room, the same way others had waited, hoping that their hearing could grow or regrow like a water lily within the walls of this aquarium?

I got up abruptly and bumped past the tall man, who was stung that I was running away from what turned out to be a meeting that my speech therapist had set up. "Weren't you telling me that you wanted to meet other hard-of-hearing people, Louise?" And then I was stammering, everything was reduced to a gob of spit that nobody could see, but that I was fixated on, eyeing its small thin droplet shape in the corner of the office like a miniature version of myself seen from outer space.

The speech therapist walked us out, energetically waving good-bye.

Then we looked at each other. Our gazes darted away from each other's eyes and mouths and hands, we turned our heads to the corners for ways out, but the street in front of us required us to head the same way. It felt like everything was heavy, as if we were bogged down in some primeval forest. I don't know which of us took the first step towards a café to "get to know each other", even if, at that point, we were already getting to know each other's avoidance tactics. Having plopped down around the café table, we couldn't disguise the fact that we were there together, each in a glass capsule. The start of our conversation was punctuated with "huh?" and "what?" as our ears turned to each other and we had a chuckle at the impression that we were mimicking each other. The waiter, rattled by our pantomime, brought us our coffees without the usual niceties, and we were both so primed for phantom questions that we launched into a tourney of absurd manners: "oh, thank you", "no problem", "all good", "that's perfect". The waiter beat a hasty retreat and we ended up laughing a little. Now, finally, we could look each other in the eye.

Like me, he had dark eyes: his iris was indistinguishable from his pupil, so that its movements towards my lips were subtle even if intense. And yet it was I who offered him my eyes, seeking out our points of similarity on his lips, convinced that our lives were framed by the same emotions and that we would be two chess grandmasters sharing our differing strategies for not losing a match.

He loved travelling while I hated it. I'd internalised how "leaving is a small form of dying." I peppered him with questions about his taste for the faraway. I'd never been able to read lips in English; all the words were swallowed up.

I always saw them disappear in the back of the mouth, borne away by saliva as if by the foam of the open sea.

Whether the flow of his words had smoothed out his voice, which became less whistling, or his ease had altered his own language, I couldn't be sure, but I could now understand everything he was telling me.

He only felt at home while abroad. Not understanding was part and parcel of being a foreigner.

"Here, all people are is annoyed and suspicious."

I nodded wordlessly.

Then he asked me if I lived on my own.

"Not really, I have a soldier and a dog and lately I've been thinking there might be someone new."

His eyes dropped to my stomach.

The misunderstanding made me giggle.

But all I said was: "I'm inhabited."

We parted ways by taking stock of our differences. He was a member of an association of people who were deaf in their left ear and had a hearing aid in their right, sponsored by Atavix – a community that, he said, had members the world over. The only association I'd ever been a member of was for children with heart conditions, just so I could push a childhood crush around in a wheelchair on the Bois de Vincennes's gravel paths.

All that meeting someone else hard-of-hearing had taught me was that he and I were no more like each other than a crested tit and a blue tit. No more like each other in how we made sense of things.

I was feeling like a bag of bones blowing in the wind, all alone and pecking at the joints holding me upright, when I noticed the gleam of a cigarette in my building's courtyard, then the profile of a lowered head, a bent back, like a tightrope walker mid-air who had to cross an abyss with a huge stinking weight, a bulky heap of trash on his back. It was the neighbour-friend.

He seemed not to recognise me. I stood in front of him and the mass I'd seen on his back. "Hello." He didn't say anything and I didn't really recognise him: his features were still there but his face had gone, his eyes weren't following me, nor was his nose or mouth. It was like I was in front of a bowl of yoghurt: I could see the indentations made by a spoon, but nothing more. I walked off straight-away. I had a distinct feeling that the huge, stinking weight I thought I'd seen was coming alive and if I looked back I would see tiny, fidgety, screeching monkeys spilling out to hurl insults at me.

The winding stairwell swallowed up this chilling image that I'd slammed the door on. In the living room, the soldier and the dog were accompanied by the woman from the herbarium. She introduced herself as a botanist. I sat down on the sofa and I heard her high-pitched voice, clear and ringing: "It can only grow in forgotten spaces, non-existent or unmapped areas."

I interrupted her: "What are you talking about?"

"The hazy pansy, *Viola vagus*," the botanist answered, before continuing. "Its chlorophyll's structure deteriorates outside its natural habitat. Thus far it has been impossible to study it outside the nebulous landscapes that make up its habitat. It only flourishes in deserted lands rich in antimatter: meteor craters, some age-old conflict zones, or cartographic fault lines."

43

My genetic test results, part of evaluating my eligibility for an implant, had come back.

There was nothing.

No illness.

No explanation for my loss of hearing or my deafness.

Not the least explanation for the flaw that caused everything to start not working.

All was still as vague as ever.

44

At my desk, I read articles about archives. There was no obligation, but inventorying the names of those recognised dead so long after the Great War had piqued my fascination, so I was poring through these columns of text as if they were life-and-death matters.

And so I'd come upon a piece titled "The Past Is Slipping Away".

It explained that attempts to archive the web had come to naught, that the past was slipping away, that the future would be even less easily recorded and preserved. The instability of mediums, their extremely brief lifespan, meant that we were plunging ever deeper into forgetfulness.

Anything I didn't make time each day to put in my sound herbarium could well be erased from my ears.

Upon returning home, I solemnly gave the herbarium pages to the botanist, placing them at her feet as if they were an offering: a complex animist ritual by which, I hoped, the sheets on which I'd inscribed the noises of daily life would, however briefly, become flesh within her and migrate back to me.

She welcomed the rite and reassured me that she would guard the sound herbarium jealously beside her miraginary plants.

The storm was brewing.

Home

Latin name: *tempestas*

Vulgar name: storm

Latitude: 48.8355906

Longitude: 2.344926100000066

Ice cap on fire.

45

I remembered the storm that shattered my childhood.

It was how the idea of an end got into my mind. This agonising feeling that something might never be as it had once been, that something could come and destroy all that was perfect in the world, transform a summer afternoon full of children's shrieks, of blades of grass stuck to eyelashes, into the darkest and loneliest of nights, into shivering in a chair of lifeless wood and into watching shadows devour the branches of trees, the bends of rivers, the roofs of houses.

That storm showed me that adults were no longer adults but lifeless dolls with heads torn off, limbs yanked out. The storm turned their faces into grimaces, their mouths into rictuses, their fillings into exposed ores. It made their eyes roll back in their heads.

"Thunder" was the word they used for this explosion or implosion of every part of the cosmos, but on the day that my childhood began to die, I wondered: Who will tell me that what's happening is real? That this word matches up to that thing? How could I be sure when nobody had ever warned me that there would be a day, there would be a moment when a storm arrived, and after that nothing would be the same, that the sun's light would fester in puddles of ice? Nobody told me a thing, nobody warned me that I would be all alone as I yelled into the midday night before their war-torn faces crosshatched by wet hair; that my childhood would go to pieces amid general indifference.

And him.

His eyes are tinted the grey of stormy nights, the grey in which I realised I could lose him as well.

46

How wonderful it would be to do nothing but draw pictures deep in a grotto to portray my love for him: he was iconic.

47

A long slow-motion avalanche was burying all my points of reference: the monster crouching deep in my ear was gorging on more and more words. The only places where I could still find Thomas's voice were in the bath and in the whispers he pressed to my ear. As I washed my body, I set my ears at the edge of the water and he, on the other end, his mouth. The reverberation of sound from his mouth travelled across the surface and the vibrations bounced against my nearly dead eardrum. It was odd: his crystal-clear voice as loud as the wind felt like nothing so much as a memory. His voice was shadowy, punctuated by the occasional splash of water. I felt like a stalagmite caught in the toils of time. I answered him, he started over again, and we talked through water. We plunged our bodies into silence; vibrations alone enveloped us. In those moments, I was Thomas's voice, and he mine, and I felt like nothing would disappear.

We often delighted in games of whispers, my ear in his mouth. As his lips pulled away, so did all sound. A game of space and soundboxes, his breath in my ear condensed and grew damp until my ear was dripping with Thomas's voice. How could I not love that image: a game of the two of us making a cloud in the overcast sky of my ear.

Our bodies brought us back to loamy soil. No words needed planting between us.

Silence had far more to teach us; it made more of us.

48

But when this silence threatened yet again to expel me from reality, it became yet again an enemy to be fought – where the soldier had gone I didn't know; he'd told me he was "on a mission", that I'd have to go it alone – and this battle had a name: Implant.

I turned the word over, this way and that:

Implant

A plan

A plant

Thomas was leaning towards "a plant". He did like the idea of a technological seed flowering in my brain and turning me to the light, like a genetically modified sunflower. Thomas was a forward-thinking sort. He wasn't afraid.

But Thomas wasn't me.

49

Anna repeated: "Cochlear implants are a capitalist war machine. Who's invested in improving man? The military! Oh, Louise, do you really want to be a fighter with advanced physiological and cognitive abilities?"

No, I shot back, of course I didn't.

She told me about nanobots connected to biological neurons controlling emotions. "That's the other reason they'll get you on an implant soon, so they can also link up to you and download knowledge. They'll dig into every nook and cranny of yours. The line between human and nonhuman is going out the window. When it comes down to it, what they want of you is the same thing they want of a machine: to be something they can control. Something they can turn off, then back on."

Anna had a point. I had to think about myself bio-ethically, figure out my personal ethics.

My days were swallowed up by articles Anna sent me about high-tech companies' goals. The pieces about implants inserted into the human brain by neurosurgical robots chilled me to the core. People could use smartphones and computers just by thinking. I told her she had it all wrong, that was for people with motor disabilities, that had nothing to do with me. No, you don't get it, you're disabled and that doesn't matter to "them". Anna was turning into a conspiracy theorist, taking a dislike to anything new. She kept insisting that the people behind technological developments were sci-fi fanatics, that getting an implant would be putting that whole world inside my body.

It wouldn't be long before they turned me into a direct interface between extremely profitable apps and my brain. Any second now they'd be able to record my thoughts, save a copy of my mental state or call an Uber for me. They could also decide that I was uninteresting or unproductive and totally change me by transferring someone else's mind into my head . . .

Enough!

I imagined myself walking through the cold after an evening at Anna's and seeing an Uber pull up, ordered and already paid for by the implant the second I'd randomly thought that I couldn't wait to be in a warm space again.

Another scenario began to haunt my nights: ending up as someone else.

One morning, a stranger would be in my bed and the stranger would be me. In my dream, Thomas wouldn't be aware of the metamorphosis; he'd go on calling me Louise. And I'd have this impression of betraying him, of having been unfaithful with this other woman who was me, whose name was different, deformed, full of strange consonants. There would be something in my throat, I would finally spit out a bit of ear full of saliva between us.

Often I woke up at that point, with that feeling of a scratchy throat, sore from reality, as if I'd been shouting into the night without ever being heard.

50

Our plates' rims were surrounded by sauce stains, crumbs and drops of wine. I was a pro at leaving traces of each thing on the table, while Thomas had a laser focus. The whole meal landed in his belly without any detours – nothing like me always losing something along the way.

Anna brushed everything away with her hands so that the remnants of breakfast, lunch, and dinner all formed a blast radius that only grew wider as she grew drunker. And, this evening, the resulting circle just about encompassed us all.

Anna and Thomas were often at loggerheads. They'd both lean over to me and explain the argument that was brewing between the two of them. Even the point of disagreement could be a matter of dispute.

In Anna's opinion, tonight's topic of conversation was multimedia storytelling while, in Thomas's opinion, the debate was around how algorithms could find answers essential for research but without any way for humans to follow their logic.

I kept my mouth shut so as not to complicate things even further.

Until a noise made us all jump: a glass shattering on the floor. I saw a calloused hand with black nails on the table, a mudslide of sound that I suspected was a string of curses. Anna glanced in the same direction I did, while Thomas went to the kitchen to get something to sweep up the mess. I noticed the soldier's curls poking above the table; he was on the ground. Anna burst out laughing and then launched into a song as she usually did. The soldier's hoarse voice joined in. I panicked: Thomas would come back. What was I going to tell him? I'd rather go find him in the kitchen and wait for the song to die down. The soldier had to leave at some point.

In the kitchen, I said all sorts of things to distract him, idiotic things like those songs, idiotic things like "you're so good to me", to cover up what was happening. Thomas was no idiot, but I did appreciate that he picked up on my unease, and my love awkwardly spilled out of my lips to keep him close.

By the time we re-emerged, the hand on the table was gone and Anna was quietly humming a country song while running a finger along the rim of her glass.

I was relieved. Thomas's knee pressed against my thigh under the table, but Anna's eyes were still fraught with a worrisome emotion.

"Did you tell Thomas?"

"Tell him what?"

I glared at Anna, silently begging her to drop it.

"Well . . ." She gestured towards the shattered glass, tilting her head and her mass of hair lecherously. "The man in your life?"

Anna was bored and in a mood to stir the pot. Her muleheadedness was trying to get the better of my level-headedness. Thomas chuckled, he had to be thinking that Anna was trying to goad me into saying words I hated like "love" and other empty nothings.

Anna's mouth opened for *l* sounds, revealing a tongue intent on dislodging crumbs stuck between her teeth. Anna's sentences were full of rounded vowels, lining her face with yet more creases, as if her mouth were the impact zone of a pebble skipped across water and her face were a set of nested ovals. Thomas's face widened in shock, then the corners of his mouth twisted, deepening the dimples of his cheeks – a sign that he disapproved of Anna's train of thought as her voluble lips darkened with the red wine's tannins. I pressed mute, turned off my hearing aid, blurred it all into nothingness, and I stared at the circle of Anna's crumbs holding us captive.

51

On the way home, Thomas didn't say anything. Or, rather, if he said something, I didn't hear it. I saw the shadow of my cursed dog, its dead eye at my heels, yelping in the darkness. Was there any connection between the soldier's missions and Anna? Why was everything just beyond my grasp? I needed explanations, even if I couldn't give Thomas any since I felt like his normality needed to be protected, like he'd never get exactly how much of a mess I was. The dog trailed us and I saw that something was off, it didn't look the same anymore. Its fur was different and its pelt seemed to be thicker, like a sheep whose wool hadn't been sheared for ages. Even its scar was hidden beneath the dark hair, its dead eye buried beneath that brown overhang.

When we got to my place, Thomas finally let out that he thought Anna was over-psychologising existence.

"This whole thing about a soldier," he said – and at those words my heart started pounding – "she really thinks you're at war, that you're under siege."

It was both a relief and a nightmare that he hadn't

147

believed Anna, that he couldn't imagine such a thing might be possible.

I wanted to bark into the night.

"What are you thinking about?" he asked me.

I was thinking about that ball of hair that kept on growing, I was thinking about how it would soon be gone if I didn't do anything.

But I answered: "The same thing you are."

Thomas gave me a sly look and turned his lips to me. I crushed mine against his. He tried to part them with his tongue while my thoughts lingered on the names of clouds. I had learned them all by heart when I was little, as a respite from the always-on television in the evenings.

"Cirrus!"

In a flash, the name of my one-eyed animal came to me. As it slipped out of my mouth, so did Thomas's tongue. Cirrus was the name of a cloud with long wisps. I rushed towards the black ball hiding beneath the kitchen table: "Cirrus! Cirrus!" My hands groped in the darkness to shake it. "Cirrus!" And I felt what might be cartilage beneath my fingers, moving cartilage. Ears, probably.

I got down: "Cirrus, I won't forget you."

52

That night, sleepless and fretting over Cirrus's fur, the soldier's excesses, and my ears making a run for it, I left Thomas in bed to find the soldier in the kitchen. To assuage my growing worry, we played rock, paper, scissors into the growing dawn. I wanted to ask him about his relationship with Anna.

Pink cumulus clouds slowly deepened the creases of our hands. Morning was tugging at the corners of our eyes. The soldier looked like a reptile: eyes hooded by fatigue, mouth a thin line, nostrils reddened by cocaine.

Under the table, Cirrus was practically unrecognisable with his fur growing almost before my eyes. No point trying to shear anything growing back this fast. Cirrus was scratching away.

And then, suddenly, Thomas came in to get some water.

He stood in the doorframe for a minute, feet on the tiles, eyes heavy with sleep, cheeks imprinted by the pillow's folds, boxer shorts galvanised by the kitchen's cold. Night and the bed had taken their toll on his body.

He didn't say a thing.

At this scene, his eyes blinked like the city's neon signs with the brightening day.

He stood there a while longer, until the light had painted the room a new colour.

I gave him an awkward wave, explained that I hadn't been able to sleep, that I wasn't alone. No point making introductions, I said in a voice that brooked no argument. Thomas didn't understand any of it; he seemed dazed.

The soldier traded looks with the botanist down the hall who was holding a sea urchin shell. She came in with a bowl of petals and offered them to all present. The soldier took a fistful, poured in some milk, and downed his bowl listlessly, while the botanist fried up the rest in birch sap.

Thomas took a seat at the table, his eyes as blank as an ice floe after an orca had gone by with a penguin in its mouth.

53

I don't know how it all looked to Thomas, if any of it had actually sunk in amid the fug of early morning, but everyone got up without a second glance to start their day. I myself was scheduled for a test with a whole array of electrodes.

I didn't know what exactly that test would consist of, but it was another step in evaluating my eligibility for an implant.

The test was at the hospital. I found Babinski again and the floor for audiograms where the soldier had turned up for the first time – he gave me a slightly disgusting wink with his ruined face.

In the hallway where I was waiting, the sounds were all muffled, as if they'd had to make their way across bone-dry, hostile expanses to reach me wearied and pallid and gaunt. All I heard of them was a single uniform wheeze.

The hospital was only hospital-like in the images it presented me with: white scrubs going by in green hall-ways, doors opening and closing, patients looking around wide-eyed so as not to miss why they were here, getting up, limping behind scrubs, disappearing on the undersides of my eyelids.

A young woman who I suspected was training for a new job after a dark career as an undertaker stood in front of the line of patients and I interrupted her as I stood up and said my name. By sheer luck, it was my turn.

She led me into a room that looked like the backdrop for a documentary about advances in medicine and had me sit on a bed with machines all around. The young doctor gestured awkwardly for me to take out my hearing aid and placed electrodes on my chest, behind my earlobes and across my forehead.

I felt the electrical currents. I felt a warmth, as if someone were striking a match under my skin. Then, for a long while, I heard whistles. I thought about the electrical shocks that were administered to those suffering trauma from the War. On the undersides of my eyelids, I saw the soldier gritting his teeth, his eyes screwed shut, his body tensed and almost arching.

Once the test was finished, the doctor came to see the results on the screen, and another, older woman joined her. They took off my electrodes as they talked to each other. I asked for a paper towel to wipe away the grainy dried gel which smelled burnt.

What had been burned within me? Memories? Like in the scenarios Anna loved telling me about? Could the memories of the sounds I'd grown up with be burned like flower bulbs that had become necrotic in the winter chill? What was being burned within me?

That was what I was obsessing over when the woman turned to me:

"You need to get an implant."

She repeated it as I stayed silent: "You need to get an implant," with a thick accent – maybe it was eastern European, but it could just as easily have been one from Burgundy.

I asked what the test had been, and what the results had been.

Her lips' movements were forced, and she released simple words: "You are deaf, very deaf. It's clear. The audiogram, your brain answers. This is the machine."

She showed me the renderings on the screen, it was like the plot of a rocky plain. The old PC showed the full picture in multiple windows that had green renderings on black backgrounds. They looked like results recorded by a probe on the Moon, they mostly showed small craters.

"But what's new here?" I asked.

"You are deaf. The machine says."

I nodded, annoyed. "Yes, I already knew that."

As the moon-landscape studies went in a folder, I fumed: two hundred years of technological progress to tell me something I'd always known.

54

I was afraid. The implant was a cold, uncaring technology – "Why uncaring?" – that would overwrite a part of me, thrust me into another world, another life that wasn't me – "But it'll still be you."

The speech therapist said: "With an implant, it'll be *different*."

What was that supposed to mean, though?

Different.

As I thought about it, I realised that this word was everywhere: on every single billboard, from menstrual pads to whisky, it circumscribed daily life, but it remained utterly mysterious.

Would I recognise my mother's voice, Thomas's voice, Anna's voice, my own voice?

The idea of not recognising my own voice plunged me into a heavy stupor. I was wracked by a visceral fear of ending up with a split personality. I imagined hearing myself as an unfamiliar voice, inhabited by someone else, being torn asunder on the inside, as if centuries had gone by in the same street without any sign, any trace.

I would be in this sci-fi setup where the world was exactly the same and yet *different*. I would look at my mother and wonder if she wasn't a machine that I was supposed to call Maman. I imagined hearing myself say "Maman" in this future.

"But you'll hear."

But what if I didn't want to hear like that? What if I rejected myself?

There would be no way to remove it. My ear would be reupholstered in metal.

I wouldn't have a natural cochlea anymore. There would be a foreign body.

I would be in a pea-soup fog and that would be called the world.

"You're overthinking it."

I turned off my hearing aid, my mother kept on talking, my eyes avoided her lips.

What if it worked?

Would I want to play team sports, understand when someone yelled, "Ball, ball, ball!", slip into dimly lit bars and make small talk, have a career in marketing, answer the phone as blithely as Cathy+, oversee teams, run brainstorming sessions, supervise others, go see films without subtitles?

That wasn't something I could imagine. As if an implant could lobotomise a social setup I'd had for twenty-five years, cement such a fracturing of my identity.

I wouldn't be fundamentally other. No, I wouldn't be more high-performing with an implant, so I said:

"Stop it, things aren't that bad."

"Louise. You're on the verge of depression."

My mother was an oxbow lake, cut off from my worries.

"You whine when the dentist puts aluminium in your cavities, but you can't get your head around why I don't want someone putting metal in my ear?" I snapped.

"You can't go on like this. If we can't talk to you then how will anything get done?"

I saw her on the continent of the hearing weeping at the sight of me setting sail for the islands of the deaf.

"You can learn sign language," I shot back at her brimming eyes.

I think I was needling her to needle myself.

On that continent were my family, Thomas, Anna, my colleagues, everybody. I'd be far from the madding crowd, letting them get on with their socioeconomic frenzy and I'd drift away on my own aboard a boat I'd made with my courage. It would float by my will. I'd cross the riptides of silence, lonely as some Robinson Crusoe deserting civilisation, naked and armed with nothing but my tenacity, flexing my puny muscles in the darkness.

After endless nights and days in this new, featureless

landscape, I would become habituated. I'd develop a taste for it, the light would be nicer, and everything would gleam in this silence, the world would have a new shine to it. I'd finally be ready to berth on deaf lands. A small community of Deaf islanders would welcome me, and we'd talk in a flower-language.

"Louise, you can't do that to me."

She'd raised her voice enough that her words were reaching me.

She turned her back to me, sobbing, drowning her distress in unthinking routine as if, by smoothing out the tablecloth, the world would go back to being this calm, comfortable space my mother could curl up in.

We were shut away in the bitterness of this thick silence of incomprehension, this dense forest in which we were both getting lost, bracing against our fears.

56

"You're on the verge of depression." My mother's words came back to me while Thomas was pan-frying some onions. I'd flipped through my sound herbarium to find the noise of slivers in fat and I found:

Home

Latin name: *cepe frixum*

Vulgar name: fried onions

Latitude: 48.8355906

Longitude: 2.344926100000066

Muttering of drunk hares.

With this imaginary soundtrack, I regained the feeling of being ensconced in days, hours, seconds, a space-time shared with others generally called "ordinary". I imagined this past spent on my islet of silence, in this swaying where all that filled the space was the wind.

I shut my eyes, and Thomas's scallop-like back, his face covered by his dark curls overhanging the pan, and the onions all vanished. My reality was reduced to the dark veil of my eyelids shot through by filaments of light.

The word that my mother had uttered, "depression",

summoned up images of my neighbour, of his hidden silhouette in the night topped by his black bag full of yowling monkeys.

I saw him through my window. For some weeks now, he had been barely sleeping, or at least at no regular hour, as far as I could tell, and when I saw him in the courtyard, he stood behind the insurmountable, shadowy wall of sleep.

Every so often he seemed to be shaken by a shudder that I attributed to some form of fear, that of having to cross realms inhabited by reality.

I felt Cirrus's fur against my calves and glimpsed, through the kitchen door, the botanist diligently peering into her microscope. With each passing day, I could make out her grainy skin sprouting large brown patches like tree bark.

Thomas sat down across from me and asked, enunciating wildly, if I was tired.

I said: "Can't I be? Aren't I a person?"

I felt like giving Thomas a hard time, dumping some acid out the window, shooting a bazooka at the clouds, tossing a grenade into the florist's, making the dog implode with microwaves.

Thomas pulled himself up and headed to the bathroom.

What could Thomas possibly be fixating on while I was in distress? I glanced at the gap in the door. I expected to see him looking at himself in the mirror, distraught, splashing his face and taking stock of the situation, but no, Thomas was standing at the sink and cleaning.

Left hand holding the water glass – right hand running the sponge clockwise all the way around – setting down the gleaming glass – wringing the sponge – wiping down the sink stopper – movements and space kept to a minimum – leaning his hips forwards, maintaining his posture.

It was so out of place, as if Thomas were folding laundry in the middle of a battlefield, repeating personal development mantras among the war dead.

At that moment I knew Thomas would help me to find a new form as a functional, reasonable thing.

57

"There's no truth. Reality is always shifting. You have to get used to that, Louise!"

I didn't like it when people said my name.

Thomas kept saying "Louise" as he tried to explain that I needed to put down my sound herbarium. He was convinced that I had to let this nostalgia go. He was tired of seeing me go through my notebooks to find the reality of existence, of seeing me hole up in the bedroom to reconstruct soundscapes from entries like "storm" + "Thomas's voice" + "fried onions" + "motorcycle" + "ringtone".

In the kitchen's harsh fluorescent light, he reeled off a long speech, his mouth wide open – I could practically count all thirty-one of his teeth.

"We don't even know what's real. If I say that this part of the window is blue" – he pointed to the kitchen dormer and waited for me to nod – "I'm telling a truth. But that's only a half truth, so it's a lie."

He paused – I nodded.

"This part of the window isn't all by itself, it's in a building, in a city, in a country."

Pause – nod.

"It's surrounded by grey, that's these cement walls. And blue, that's the sky, the clouds, plenty of other things."

Pause – nod.

"And if I don't say everything, absolutely everything, I'm lying. But saying everything is impossible, even when it comes to this window, this little sliver of physical reality."

Pause – nod. But where was he going with this? My ability to concentrate was waning quickly.

"Reality has no limits and if I forget a single thing, I'm lying."

Pause – nod.

"For humans, this reality changes all the time."

"Yes," I said.

"We already aren't what we were just a few minutes ago."

I recalled my frustration, my anger from a few minutes ago and, yes, I wasn't the same now.

His stormy grey eyes were wide, his arms formed an arc above me, his fingers spread apart. In this gesture I got the feeling that his next words were a cry:

"Forget how you hear, what's real is what you'll hear with an implant!"

58

I needed to believe that I had a choice.

First of all, I wanted to go see the Deaf side, see what life was like there, see whether I could join them rather than get an implant.

I registered for a sign language class taught by a Deaf professor at an association promoting Deaf culture.

The teacher was profoundly deaf, and we were absolutely not allowed to use our mouths, only our hands and our facial expressions. We were so awkward, our fingers stuck together, the gestures halting. We had to start over again and again. We were like clumsy, frustrated children, even a bit brainless in blandly trying without any imagination to turn our ideas into signs.

Suddenly, a chair fell over, and the teacher and I turned at the same time, a second after the four other students who were hearing. This tiny happening made me realise that we had the same auditory baggage.

"Without my hearing aid, I hear like you," I signed to him as best as I could.

"Maybe," he answered, "but you are hearing, you

went to a hearing school. I'm Deaf, I've been signing since I was little, we'll never be the same."

In fact, our dialogue was more like this:

"If no device, me same you hear," and him: "Maybe, but you hearing, you talk, me deaf. Different. Why? You to school hearing, me to school deaf. Me sign child."

In the way he signed "different", emphatically striking one finger against the other and pairing the arabesque made by his right forefinger's motion with a shrug of the shoulders, I sensed contempt. He made it clear that the two of us belonged to dissimilar worlds: he to the one of capital-D Deaf people who signed, and I to that of lowercase-d deaf – oral – people who talked.

He saw me as a turncoat.

I tried to explain that I was going to become *totally* deaf, even more deaf than him, but I got the feeling that my protests only deepened the pride he took in his caste. He hated newcomers or those trying to join the community belatedly. I hadn't grown up with a forbidden language, hadn't been forced to talk unwillingly, and of course a childhood like that marked one for life.

The Deaf laughed at "talking oral folks" with monkey-like grimaces. Our ungainly mouths had no reach while their signs ferried so, so many images.

The creativity of sign language, the integration of body and physical space were a contrast to the constraints of the French language. In the stories they told – freed from a hidebound grammar, with simple tense markers – plot and character and nuance, not to mention the commentary all around, erupted before the eye with a virtuosity that left us mouth-talkers scrambling. We felt suddenly conscious of our stony faces, our bodies weighed down by years of orality. We were so awed that, in unison, we bemoaned the misery of mouths and voice exercises, the weight of sentences.

The teacher had us play a game where we were in a storm on the open sea; to survive we had to pick someone to throw overboard. Everyone chose to keep a Deaf person aboard because, amid the wind and the waves, there was no jettisoning a Deaf person's sign language and keen eyes.

"You didn't choose your own side!" the teacher observed, signing each "ha" of his laughter.

The sign for "choose" mimed a thing being plucked and it perfectly encapsulated this feeling that an invisible hand had pulled me out of a haze and decided on the place I now found myself: the world of the hearing.

"But I didn't choose." I wanted to convince the teacher.

This hand in the word "choose" was the hand of so many generations that had all wanted each of its members to adapt to norms, and the norm was the French language. "In the beginning was the Word" had spotlighted oral deaf people with their "talking mouths", their unmoving bodies and impassive faces, hence those hours of speech therapy learning how to read lips and recognise words by ear, hear better, hours perfecting my speech to sound normal, hours learning vocabulary, being impeccable with my grammar, all that so as not to be relegated to a category that I didn't belong to, Deaf, and so as not to appear to be someone that I actually wasn't.

"You've built up a whole life as one of 'them,'" the teacher added.

But I didn't feel like I belonged to the world of the hearing.

He made another gesture, the back of his hand flat against his forehead, his middle finger touching his thumb before flicking out: that was how I learned the word "denial" in French Sign Language. I'd expelled from my thoughts the deaf woman who, deep down, I was. Shame was written on my face.

My mind was on that when an argument broke out: the Deaf teachers were inviting us to join a protest against getting every deaf person an implant. French healthcare was now fully covering the high cost of implants for newborns, and the Deaf community saw that as a threat to their culture, as political will further encroaching upon their way of life.

My unease about getting an implant only grew with that information. Where would I belong, then? Who was I? The idea of my actual self receded, transformed, this *something* that I was had now been reduced to my personal information, to what was on my ID card:

Louise F., born on 21 June 1990, in Champigny-sur-Marne, brown eyes, 1.63 m tall. Issued by the Malbranche prefecture.

That was the only stable part of this *something* that was me.

59

Back at my flat, the botanist offered me her latest find: the foamy narcissus.

What was special about this miraginary plant was its lack of any flowering system. It was handicapped by a backwash of bitterness.

"Spume plays the same role that an enzyme does and breaks down the narcissus's endogenous components. The foamy narcissus as such is unable to manifest as a flower and to play a role within an ecosystem."

60

My mother had me over for dinner and, in the kitchen, she had her serious look on. When I was little, I thought it was a secret mask.

When she wore her serious look, I knew I had to focus to lip-read what she was going to tell me. I hated being held hostage by what she had to say. I had to pull out all the stops to avoid having to ask her to repeat herself unless I wanted to see her eyes fill up with tears. When my mother had that face on, it was a flashing red warning and my deafness had to lie low.

I stood and met her asymmetric face head-on. I could see her nostrils flare with emotion. My mother furrowed her brow even further, a sign that the words were coming. The kitchen was where everything my mother absolutely had to say came out and even the floating motes of dust picked up the light like fireflies to illuminate her lips. Every organ in my body was hanging on what she had to say. Her upper lip rose, her nostrils narrowed as she inhaled.

"You shouldn't" – her lips puckered, there was definitely a run of *oo*'s and *m*'s or *p*'s, and by the way her tongue was tapping against her teeth there had to be *t* or *d* consonants, her lips quivered with emotion and distorted the clear shape of words. I still managed to pick out the word "ever" and then "get an implant".

The word "implant" was a one-two punch: the jab of the first syllable, a brief inhale, then the uppercut of the lips forcing out a *p* followed by the sight of the tongue's blue-veined underside and the quick exhale of the second syllable. I lip-read it everywhere, all the time, and feared it. It sent an icy shiver down my neck that continued as a cascade into my thoughts.

My mother's eyes were fixed on mine, waiting worriedly for my reaction, her fingers trembling in her hair, along her necklace, increasing her tension, the sentence's, and mine.

"You shouldn't ever get an implant."

How selfish could my mother get? She was full of contradicting orders; she'd never got past the stage where a child was merely an extension of herself. Everything that happened to me was an affront to the natural order of our relationship. That was what I thought, and couldn't say to her questioning eyes and her closed lips.

Of course I'd get an implant. I'd be her child with an implant, a damn plug in my head, a cyborg.

"No, no, Maman. No. I'm going to get an implant!" I finally let out. The words escaped my throat. They hurt to say but they still came out, white-hot, full of fear.

My mother froze completely. Her arms were like the forelegs of a praying mantis, her head was slightly tilted away, her round right eye was on me as the other one, caught in the crest of her nose, was doing its best to assess the situation.

I made some sort of movement that knocked over a chair. My dismay had my arms and legs going every which way. I opened my mouth. She caught me.

"Louise, you didn't understand me."

That I could understand. It was a stupid thing to say.

She grabbed my wrist, positioned herself in front of me, and repeated, making it clear that I was to repeat what she said. I could feel her fingers' pressure on my wrist: we were both shaking, I felt so fragile and I could tell she was utterly helpless.

"I said."

"You said."

"You should."

"I should."

"Meet."

"Meet."

My mother nodded.

"People."

"With implants." I finished the sentence for her.

We looked at each other in relief.

61

Every misunderstanding sapped my strength. Every word I didn't understand became another injustice. Never mind that I leaned forwards, looked carefully at lips, opened my eyes wide, had my inner lexicographer ready to go, steeled my nerves, and told myself "you'll get this sentence" – failure seeped into every part of my existence.

The world was far too fast-paced, heads and hands were constantly moving, making it harder to read lips.

And worst of all were evenings.

I hated those the most.

As those came, the peaks and valleys of faces dissolved, blurring into a two-dimensional world, and people kept on talking and guffawing in the waning day.

Light was my ally, it let me pick up the nuances of lip and tongue movements; in the half-darkness, all the nooks and crannies of words were lost, all that remained was the carcass, more or less: open mouths, closed mouths, nothing more.

Even in mid-afternoons, I felt worry coming on. I glanced nervously at the sky and the impending night.

In a panic, I took in the human beings around me and felt trapped within their communications. I tried to free myself from the snares of their lips. I wanted to run away and be home, but I had to wait and smile politely at my colleagues who were also wending their way to the day's end, heading for the bus or the Métro without a second thought.

At dusk, with the satisfaction of a day behind them, my colleagues bellowed, brightened up, mentioned one thing or another, interrupted each other, and I felt the questions glance off my shoulders, the laughs like blows to my gut.

Their bewilderment or unmoved stares made me shiver. Pulled into their supposedly infectious joy, I gave evasive answers, talked about rubbing, humming, plumbing, I opened my mouth wide to laugh with them, let out a "Clearly!" when everything around me was less and less clear.

Each day, there was a stretch before the streetlights came on, a few long minutes when the fluorescent lights crackled, lit up in fits and starts before illuminating the ends of sentences that I could catch if I still had some strength left to piece together the puzzle.

"Don't forget the borough, Louise!"

"Don't forget to borrow, Louise!"

"Don't forget tomorrow, Louise!"

But maybe they hadn't been saying my name all the while. Maybe they'd been saying the word for "hearing":

"Don't forget, tomorrow, *l'ouïe*!"

I wavered between "You got it!" and "Don't worry!" or the always-handy "What?" – but I didn't want to give that last one yet another go.

I'd worn that to pieces.

And besides, they were already gone.

62

I had to go to the Babinski building again to discuss the eligibility evaluation that had been undertaken after the audiogram of the hearing test. On the Métro, voices crashed against my body. My skin bristled at the sight of those mouths and became as prickly as a hedgehog's when I felt their breath run across my forearms and my face.

I associated human beings with sandstorms. The city's streets had turned into a Death Valley and I moved through it as a shield-body against hot breaths and onslaughts of sound.

Their mouths had become small scurrying monsters whose appendages consisted of the tongue, a somewhat pointy and somewhat pink head of sorts crowned by the undulating scalp of the palate which was rarely seen and, to the back, the uvula, a dangling and pulsing brain that sometimes shook under the blows of extreme vowels: *i, u, a*.

As I waited before my appointment and saw the corners of mouths tense for short *i*'s and mock-happy eyes accompanying that movement, I daydreamed about that vowel's shrillness. The consonants accompanying it would bring the lips crashing together like cymbals or, on the contrary, deepen the long folds striating this singular skin.

After sitting for so long in the ORL hallway, I'd developed a theory about the relationship between the surfaces of lips and the shapes of teeth. I'd noticed that smooth red lips augured "offensive" teeth that were sharp or serrated, while velvety lips that were covered with a light, almost furry layer revealed a "gentle" denture: round teeth, gleaming enamel. The other half of my theory was based on what I figured was a general law since time immemorial: to always pretend to be what one isn't in order to survive. The vulnerability of bare, unprotected lips actually hid fierce teeth, while raw lips, protected by chapping, hid weak teeth that were merely ceremonial. Humans were full of tricks for subduing others and, mouth by mouth, I saw through this whole charade.

But I couldn't avoid them: mouths were everywhere.

Closed lips that had me worried that they might open.

I wanted to seal all these mouths shut.

To flee all the trouble they gave me.

I was the last one left on the hallway bench when a man came to get me. I followed his green Crocs.

He asked me how I was doing, if the evaluation tests had gone smoothly. His voice was rich, resonant, sharp. His thin lips were perfectly symmetrical.

Here, reading lips was like a slow-motion game of Tetris.

After making sure I could understand him well, he explained why it was important for people becoming profoundly deaf to get an implant as soon as possible.

"The neurons originally meant for hearing will be reused or repurposed for other senses such as sight, smell, or touch, that's what we call neuroplasticity."

I imagined my brain like a huge recycling plant for plastic neurons.

He continued: "Deafness arises when the cilia are damaged and no longer stimulate the neurons. When they're no longer regularly stimulated, the neurons that typically receive those signals atrophy and die."

I nodded: my brain had turned into a huge leper colony.

"Fortunately, even in cases of a total loss of hearing and especially when it's recent, some of those neurons survive and stay connected to the cochlear nucleus's receiving areas. If the implanted electrodes' currents manage to set off action potentials in the surviving neurons, hearing can be restored."

I was an ideal candidate: my auditory neurons were still active, and I was relatively young.

So he encouraged me to seriously consider this solution that was a cochlear implant.

There wasn't much time to decide.

Of course I could ask him questions. But I had nothing to ask.

All I wanted was to be by myself at the top of some mountain in the Himalayas wrestling with a little can of tuna.

63

On the internet, the testimonials from those about to get an implant all highlighted this terrible exhaustion that had besieged them in the days or weeks before they'd made their decision.

They all said they'd hit rock bottom.

64

The light was so bright I couldn't see. Winter had turned the building's walls white and Thomas's eyes were verging on black. The prospect of spending a whole day tripping over words was soul-sucking. I wanted to hit the stop button and let everyone, starting with myself, forget about me. Thomas's hand tugged at me like a lead until we both slowed down, as if a wild animal were sleeping nearby.

My neighbour was sitting on the bench in the courtyard and I saw the monkeys again, in his hair. His eyes like a sailboat washed up by me and I felt his sheer inertia contaminating me. There was only the anvil of his gaze, no gleam to it. Thomas yanked me out of my immobility, I felt his clammy fingers slip out of my hand, his neck stiffen. He walked straight ahead to get away from the morose scene.

Once I caught up to him, he said he'd felt something that didn't sit well with him. Had he seen the crazy monkeys? Had he seen the inertia overcome me?

I was terrified of becoming like the neighbour.

"What happened there?" Thomas asked.

Maybe he'd seen.

I promised him I'd never seen monkeys atop my head.

He didn't understand.

65

In my colleagues' eyes, my presence was ghostly. My features blurred within the building's space, while I saw them through a filthy, clouded pane of safety glass. Only a few cheek kisses touched my face, reminding me that this world was indeed the one in which I was advancing.

I never could have imagined what happened next.

In my office, without any warning, a woman whose head was a tangle of curls had been put beside my workstation. I stood in the doorway, lost for words, as she looked up and awkwardly raised a hand to wave hello.

She immediately went back to sorting a pile of death certificates into colour-coded folders. I sat down at my computer only to see a whole army of markers scattered across the desk. Yellow and red and blue and green were practically blasphemous in the archive room's monochrome. And this woman was a disco ball: everything gleamed, from her earrings to the rhinestones on her trainers. Next to her, I looked like a statue, deaf and mute.

I had nothing better to do than turn on my computer and read an email from earlier that day informing me of a change in position "consistent with my needs." *Consistent with my needs*, how could they know what my needs were when I myself didn't? My job suited me well enough: the dead were as deaf as I was.

At the end of the morning, the HR assistant showed me to my new office. I had spent the previous hour watching in stupefaction as my replacement and her curls swung this way and that over pink, blue, and green folders with her glitter pens and her intent face. I imagined she must be as passionate about getting the dead to the hereafter as about saving dolphins from dolphinariums.

At eleven o'clock I left the long hallway to plunge even deeper into the building's bowels towards another very small cell. The HR assistant left me there after giving me a sheet of paper. It outlined the procedures of my new job. I was now dealing with "undocumented people" who, for one reason or another, were missing or had never had personal records – bureaucratically stateless, as it were.

I was reminded of an article in the *Anarchist Neuro-science Review* on the "Zacchary Broch" method and this odd community of those uprooted from their language:

In 1913 Zacchary Broch was born in Bucharest to unknown parents. Orphaned and deprived of any mother tongue, he grew up filthy and mute. In 1940 he narrowly avoided deportation. Ten years later, he was found in Paris on rue Boyer in the

20^e arrondissement at the opening of an exhibition of stateless painters. He was noticed by Louise Kahn, a researcher in behavioural biology – the precursor of neuroscience – who saw him as an embodiment of linguistic uprooting. She named a language school after him for those who didn't speak language; the "Zacchary Broch" method was born. The curriculum included overtone-stutters; navel-thinking; heat-smell; contact-language. Her goal was to do away with the concept of a mother tongue by furnishing oneself with the missing language. But Zacchary Broch's relative success forced him to become a naturalised Frenchman. He rejected such prospects of a future in biological terms and, in 1961, jumped into the Seine. To pay homage to this act, the linguistically uprooted still sail to this day, forming small communities around the world.

66

As the "undocumented people" job didn't entail a significant amount of data to deal with, I was switched to part-time.

Worst of all, I couldn't even bring myself to care. I actually forgot to tell Mathilde at noon.

When I informed Thomas, he was disgusted, his face puffed up like a tarpaulin in the wind. I didn't listen to him, I simply watched fury reshape his features. He sucked in what little rage and sense of injustice remained in me.

He was especially upset by my apparent lack of concern. He finally spat out that I needed to put up a fight. All of a sudden everything lethargic in me tensed. My eyes looming high above my minaret-like neck went back to reading everything.

"It's illegal," he kept saying.

The next day, I emailed HR to file a grievance. But all I got was a sign-language interpreter who could go with me to the staff canteen and to biannual meetings.

Anna thought it was nice. She pointed out that it was

free training in sign language. I could teach her. Thomas didn't say anything; it infuriated him to see me being so passive. He was stung by this image of a second-class disabled person that I was being trapped within.

67

Did I have a choice? "You always have a choice," Anna would have said. But Anna was hearing, even though she, too, was in a slump. She saw in me a perfect exile buddy and dreamed of turning me into a modern-day hermit. She was as nuts as I was, she set off all my spectres of trauma. How would I get anywhere with Anna holding me back?

My mother was proud of having given me a subscription to the *Anarchist Neuroscience Review*. There was even a special issue about future technologies – implants might someday be able to record a whole life's worth of conversations, a black box in case of a crash.

Thomas was over the moon about accompanying a bionic being on the route to transhumanism.

As for my colleagues, I could see from their reactions that I was now severely on the disabled side: all traces of suspicion had given way to newfound empathy. Even the birth certificates team was now smiling at me in the canteen; Cathy+ had been elected staff representative and she tried to make amends in the self-service line. I guess I could say that this new dimension of clear disability, "real" disability, had the advantage of putting their minds at ease.

The soldier was using drugs more and more often and punctuating his sentences with "sweetie", his eyes manic, his body thin as a rail. The botanist with her tree-bark skin showed me her latest find. I listened to her explanation of shy-budded blackeyes with Cirrus in my lap.

According to the botanist, this plant was the most paradoxical one in nature. It was practically scared of itself, keeping its buds so far apart that they never touched.

This phenomenon of botanical shyness had been proposed by researchers but up to this point only ever observed in the crowns of trees. The quirk of climbing plants was that they coiled in on themselves in order to reach greater heights, but this variant of botanical shyness put it at odds with such coiling and therefore itself.

And where did that leave me?

68

The *Anarchist Neuroscience Review* had a whole section devoted to the linguistically uprooted. A psychopaediatrician specialising in linguistics and phonology had set out to analyse the cries and inarticulate sounds of a set of developmentally delayed children and had reached the conclusion that each one drew on speech components of various languages – English *th*'s, Spanish rolled *r*'s, Arabic guttural *r*'s, German *ch*'s.

In this way he proved that all human beings fundamentally had the ability to enunciate not only all existing languages but all possible languages, and that as they learned their mother tongues, they lost the phonemes they didn't use.

The conclusion left me bewildered: our language was richer when we didn't have mother tongues.

And so I daydreamed about other prospects to avoid thinking about getting an implant. Maybe by going completely deaf, by forgetting my mother tongue, I could find this universal linguistic source?

69

Anna ended up telling me she'd rather spend time with the soldier than with me and Thomas. She said we were like a cookie-cutter couple – and what did that leave her to dream about? "You've become so materialistic with this whole implant thing." She said I'd lost my poetry, that I was as dull as real life.

"You're too realistic," she said.

"But there's no such thing as *too* realistic, Anna. Reality is what *is*."

"If reality is all you think about, then that's depressing."

It annoyed me that she was disappointed. All this energy I'd put into hoisting myself up to all the decibels, clawing back the world's intelligibility, making it less opaque by way of sound lists – "sugar", "question", "canal", "plaster", "see-saw", "sobbing", "carrot", "ticket", "oven", "sorry", "hello" – and into beating back my fear of a cochlear implant. What right did she have to be angry with me?

Anna didn't like anything that smacked of happy endings. She wanted my whole body to reject the implant and for me to drive off into the sunset with the device rusting in the salt and the wind.

She ended up telling me that she and the soldier thought alike.

"About what?" I asked.

"Success, for example. We like people who haven't succeeded, we think success is vulgar."

I wasn't going to respond to that. I told myself that Anna considered profound deafness a lifeline.

"Yes, Louise, what would a country be like if everyone was successful? So many people failing is what's saved humanity."

I wasn't listening anymore, my eyes were lost in the distance. I'd turned off my hearing aid.

"But why is the soldier being evasive?" I asked. That was the only thing I really wanted to know. Our friendship was falling apart.

"Sometimes he's tired of looking for miraginary plants, he can't stand it, it's pointless, it's useless, he likes reality better."

That was Anna's answer.

70

As I opened the door to my flat, I stepped on bits of paper that covered the floor halfway across the living room. All the sheets of my sound herbarium had been ripped up and the pages with miraginary plants as well.

Cirrus was frothing at the mouth, spinning around, his tail slapping every corner of the room. Nothing could stop him.

I looked for the soldier amid the carnage so he'd stop with the mess. He turned up, staggering, done up in one of my sundresses. The straps were slipping down his shoulders, the pattern stretched across his too-wide chest. He was humming one of Anna's songs. The few words that sallied forth from the guttural, rough bass had been worn down by alcohol, swallowed up in the darkness of his throat. He downed his words more often than uttered them. His song was the rewound soundtrack of pre-language.

The botanist wasn't moving anymore, her skin was entirely covered in bark. She had metamorphosed into a tree in winter.

I suddenly felt overwhelmed, in a thousand pieces, with nothing to cling to. At the sight of my crestfallen face and my trembling hands, the soldier pulled off the dress. Now he looked like nothing, a gaunt silhouette, and I thought how that was a perfect likeness of my psychic state, this ruined, backlit form, with a shattered backbone.

Cirrus spun around again as the final strips of paper floated to the ground, and was gone with the soldier, leaving me all alone at the crack of dawn amid the white tatters of my ruined identity, this herbarium, this nostalgia for my long-gone ears gone in the darkest of silence.

71

NILS OYAT, HETEROGENESIS EXPERT.

I recalled the photo of that sign.

Under "heterogenesis", the dictionary said: "The birth or origination of a living being otherwise than from a parent of the same kind."

The definition could have been absolutely anything, I didn't care, I just needed help and I had an address, that was all I could ask for.

As I pushed open the heavy green door at Nils Oyat's address, I naturally didn't expect to find myself suddenly face to face with the man himself, also about to open the door.

Nils Oyat didn't look the least bit like some expert, he looked more like a middling insurance broker. He took the hand he'd been shaking and showed me around his "office", a tidy space set up like a TV studio, with rattan armchairs on both sides of a table within a huge empty room that was white with fluorescent light.

I settled into one of those chairs and told him about going deaf, this progressive loss, the appearance of a dog, a soldier, and a botanist, each one's illness, each one's misdeeds down to my sound herbarium's destruction, and the prospect of getting an implant.

His voice was confident as he suggested bringing everyone in: we could sort things out, isolate symptoms, find appropriate solutions for everyone.

"Let me assure you that I've seen all sorts. People who are poor or blind or mute or epileptic or para- or quadriplegic, folks with cancer, babies with macro- or microcephaly, children and grandchildren of the Algerian War, people who have flat feet or asthma or bad breath, scapegoats, stammerers, sculptors with hands cut off, shy salespeople, premature ejaculators, Oedipal types."

Everything he said was subtitled in yellow on a screen in front of me. Nils Oyat was the man for the job.

He spoke behind a polished façade, his voice steady, his gestures honed like a politician's, conveying openness and self-assurance.

Then he encouraged me to come stand behind a plexiglass lectern and, like on a TV show, the soldier came in without a sound, behaving himself. His curls gelled flat against his scalp made him look even odder and the oversize jacket he wore added to his downtrodden bearing. As he approached, I could see the makeup glistening on his skin. Under the bright light, he looked like a dolled-up cadaver. He stood apprehensively at his lectern and immediately rattled off disorganised memories:

"There was still thirty-five kilometres to go, three days at full speed through the valley, with the bloated corpse reeking for kilometres all around, full of all sorts of putrefying fluids. More than thirty-five kilometres, more than three days at full speed, with any luck, yes, more than thirty-five kilometres."

At this torrent and with his mangled speech on the screen, I realised that he was completely coked up.

"Would you say that you feel like you're on the edge?" Nils Oyat asked. "Could you say what it is that's keeping you from getting to where you ought to be?"

The soldier told the story of the nails in his shoes that he'd pried out to carve a name on his friend's grave. Not hearing himself walk was proof he didn't exist anymore. All he could do was snort cocaine to feel a little alive.

"Are you aware of what this substance is called by some people?"

"No."

"'Stardust.' And are you aware that an unknown author, when asked if he believed that civilisation had a future, answered yes, as he believed that man was the only animal species whose genius spoke to the stars?"

"A writer?" He blew a raspberry. "Artists can always start something imperfect over again. Life isn't like that, there's no rewriting or tossing out what we've been through. There's the rub."

"There's an opening, and you've figured it out through

stardust, although, if I may appeal to your imagination, it's a beneficial thing. I'm speaking of symbolic reparation. What sets us apart from animals is our imagination. Would you say that you feel as if you owe a debt to those who are dead?"

"Yes."

Nils Oyat concluded that the soldier had holey tongue syndrome.

"What's wrong with his tongue?" I asked.

"Not *his* tongue, the tongue we speak. It's holey. Full of holes."

I mulled that over for a long while and figured that if silence was a part of language, then, being part of one's tongue, the two couldn't be at odds.

Silence was a place to be in language. Silence set free words and images held captive by language. I hadn't gone astray, then. I was on the right track.

72

Two men brought in a wheelbarrow containing the botanist turned into a tree trunk, and set her in front of a lectern between me and the soldier.

Our bewilderment notwithstanding, Nils Oyat's tone was calm. "Let me assure you that trees can be immortal."

"But she can't talk anymore," I said.

"She has to be taken as a presence that unearths what is captive within us."

The soldier and I looked at each other and suddenly I sensed that we were both terrified to be sharing a stage with a snake-oil salesman. But Nils Oyat had a piercing gaze that allayed fears and set us at ease again.

"As we cannot question our guest directly, could you tell me about her?"

So I described how we had met and her miraginary plants.

"The last one was the alastic lichen. It's a plant with a reproductive system that doesn't function through spores, as other non-budding plants might, but by sighs of 'alas.' I think this is my favourite one, but the botanist had to abandon her research because of some sort of psychiatry—"

"Her psyche is a tree," Nils Oyat cut in. "So is the rest of her now."

I ignored his overcorrection and kept going:

"I gave her my sound herbarium."

"I'm curious about this herbarium."

"That was where I set down sounds as I heard them before losing them. They were tracks I laid down so I could follow them back to sound . . . but Cirrus destroyed them along with the botanist's flowers."

"Tracks, tracks – we should be talking about *cracks*! If your voice cracks that's just your voice's timbre changing, but if *you* crack, you lose it. You were this close to a total crack-up, but your dog saved you."

"Are you implying I'm out of my mind?"

"No, no. I'm saying that you've got to get out of your vines."

"But plants are intelligent, you know. That's what everyone says nowadays. The sound herbarium was my own little sense collection. I mean, that's how I made sense of what I'd lost. It was how I could reconstruct ambiances of sound from the past."

"That's true. However, the herbarium is made from dried flowers, plants that are dead."

"Well, if you look at them, they make you feel alive."

"On the contrary. We are only alive if we can be unsure;

we can cultivate the plants of our lives as carefully as we wish, but they'll still be overrun by face-plant after face-plant. The world of sound is full of doubt, and you have to let yourself be alive to that again."

I didn't quite follow, so I asked:

"Why did the botanist turn into a tree?"

"Because you've got yourself stuck, rooted in your presences of trauma."

73

"And now we come to symbolic reparation by ant therapy. What separates us from animals and plants is our imagination. Life is a symbolic theatre and ants help us to mend our internal stage set."

"Ants?!"

The soldier's question showed up in all caps on the subtitle screen.

"Yes, they're what most resembles us, a social organisation in which everyone has a role to play."

The soldier spat in disgust. "Social organisations are nothing but masks. Masks that life sticks on us to go with our roles. But when we're alone, absolutely alone, when there isn't a soul, not a single damned soul to see us, then what masks do we have on?"

"It is for this reason that bonds must be formed anew, to play a role with yourself, through the ants, to learn how to play without any mask, within yourself, for yourself," Nils Oyat answered. His eyes shone; he was exhilarated by the turn this conversation had taken.

"Bug therapy, bah! Who cares, we're all going to end up

in the guts of bugs anyway. Worms, maggots chowing down on our carcasses . . ."

"And yet ants have a better reputation than flies. In the Talmud, they are a symbol of honesty. In Tibetan Buddhism, they signify how pathetic materialism is. You have my word that ant therapy is tried and true because ants resist everything. There are records saying that, in 1945, the only things to survive the nuclear blasts were ants."

74

I only had a few days left to decide whether or not to get an implant. The operation had to be scheduled, there weren't many open slots, the clock was ticking.

I remembered the psychologist's line while I was at the hospital: "Your brain will have forgotten what 'before' means."

Everything would be rebuilt from the ground up.

I imagined Thomas's hand on the plug in my head, the crackling noise of his fingers running through my hair, his metallic voice asking me: "How's things?" and me answering in a whistling voice: "They're good, my love, they're very good."

The city's sounds would hammer my skull right by my ears, as if I were the spot where all the cars come in off the Périphérique, but I would hear Thomas again, talking about our new soundproofed flat, his eyes on a swallow whose spring song accompanied the waning day.

I asked Thomas: "Do you think I'll be happy with an implant?"

He looked at me with mild terror, then laughed and said I should be dealing with my axis.

"Huh? Axis? Are you trying to tell me I'm off-kilter?"

He handed me the printout I needed for my taxes.

Ant therapy had begun. Nils Oyat was assigning tasks.

He entrusted the botanist, by means of the dog, with the task of bringing out an ant species that could eat away at vines and detach them from the host, namely me.

And the therapist gave the soldier orders that amounted to rescuing an ant from a battlefield.

"Ants prepared to die on the front lines are silent," Nils Oyat explained, "and it's that call you need to hear."

I started thinking that Nils Oyat had to be the craziest of us all, with his antsanity.

I waited for my instructions but he stopped there.

"What about me?" I finally asked.

"You? Here, we treat symptoms."

While my symptoms were for the ants to treat, I went on with my actual life: work allowed me not to think too much, short-circuited my anxiety. In the staff canteen, my colleagues saved me a spot at their table but their awkward smiles flitted through my brain like birds of ill omen.

I smelled like wet dog, my breath like underbrush. I had to make a decision. It was mine alone and yet completely beyond me. The choice I was going to make would change the course of my existence and I had no way of knowing whether I would be able to say, later, "That was the right call."

"Everything will turn out fine," my mother said.

How could she be so sure of it? How could everyone not even wonder a little?

I was hearing.

I was deaf.

More hearing than deaf, because I could fill language's holes with language.

But is hearing having access to language?

Yes. And no.

Because hearing wasn't listening. The same way that looking wasn't seeing. I knew how to listen, but I didn't hear anymore. And yet, all this while, I'd been hearing language.

I'd listened to myself listening, and maybe that was where I'd gone totally deaf. By getting an implant, I'd be able to hear again and stop listening to myself listening. That was a possibility I couldn't ignore.

I wrote down:

1. We can look at seeing; we can't hear hearing.

2. We can see looking. But can we hear listening?

I tore up the paper, then I called the hospital.

"I've thought about it. The pre-implantation assessment was positive. So I'd like to get an implant."

77

Nils Oyat had me come in for a one-to-one interview.

"I've got absolutely no hope left."

"Is that so?" He looked at me knowingly, but I didn't feel like I really knew anyone, or anything.

"Man is a being full of hope and hopelessness," he went on, "if he was always wracked by hopelessness, then everyone would go to pieces. As it's illogical to hold out hope in this world we live in, that's the very proof that man is an illogical being. For something so absurd as hope to spring eternal just goes to show that you will get through this, and that it won't be by your logicality but your illogicality that you get through this situation. Make good use of it to keep going. Don't look at the logical side of things, Louise – dig into where there isn't any logic for the strength to grow. Seeing the world full of holes is by far the best thing that could have happened to you because, in reality, we know nothing about ninety-five percent of the matter in the universe. We only know that it isn't made up of atoms, that it isn't made the way we and the stars are, and this unknown mass, this huge hole, can be a metaphor for everything that escapes our being. This holey language will never be deciphered completely. So you have to accept this void to make your way down our paths without crutches."

Nils Oyat explained this need I'd had to let spectres of trauma coil like vines around me to build the bridge I was standing on. But that, now, I needed to be rid of them.

The soldier, the botanist, and the dog would have to go unless I wanted to disappear.

It was them or me.

78

"The story of the Seven Years' War, in America's heartland, a girl lived like cotton, had to follow the forest with a Paul."

An exclamation from Thomas; a quip from my mother.

I didn't try to make heads or tails of it; I let the words go by. I'd decided to stop worrying about anything. I'd grown tired of asking questions, of clarifying what I didn't understand, of listening all over again to another line that came out to make sense of the first one, of cycling through all possible interpretations. I wanted one last vacation from my senses before I got the implant. Letting go before the obstacle course that awaited me. Having no horse in this race, allowing words to swarm me one last time before I would have to hunt them down, before I would be logged by figures clad in scrubs as I raced to collect them.

"Tell them silently, like sweeteners."

I poured myself some Fanta with a giggle.

"Emilien Dussan, back swallowed."

I imagined the body of a man engulfed by the baleen of a whale.

"A crab breaks and the carash of a fable."

I floated in these images of a garage at the bottom of the sea (or of the city of Carthage), Thomas's crab-fingers intertwined with mine, my mother's mouth open, revealing lipstick traces on her teeth.

My mother's sobs of laughter bounced off the walls, died as they made contact with the fork in her mouth. Thomas's lips pursed as he looked at me. Maybe he was annoyed at seeing me sitting back, my body draped across the chair, my fingers limp, so passive. What he couldn't know was that this capitulation was fleeting. For the first time, I was getting some pleasure out of it, the lava-flows of sound floating in the air. I leaned into the vibrato of Thomas's voice as if it were hot sand and its sallies into higher pitches made my eyes jump like sea gleams. Out of the corner of my eye, I saw his uneven chewing – jaw left, jaw right – and my mother's heavy-lidded eyes indicating that she was at ease.

For the first time, I didn't envy them, understanding everything effortlessly: they had to be tired of it.

For the first time, the life of the hearing struck me as drab.

"The shame pays."

"We weld," my mother said.

"We'll toast *after* it's done."

Thomas had enunciated carefully, facing me, repeated himself until I understood.

"So you hear the bubbles."

I thought: Can people hear bubbles popping?

79

The morning of the operation, my teeth were chattering. The warmth of Thomas's body was no help, it was a journey I had to make on my own, I was all alone in the wide sea, my body frozen by the loss of an island of sound. I was like a castaway waiting for a boat to get back to land, terrified of not recognising it. The early gleam of day on the sheets, Thomas's puffy eyes, the flat's tile floors weren't enough to make things familiar again.

I didn't like endings. Finishing a dish, a cup of tea, felt impossible to me. I always contemplated myself in the last of the coffee grounds. To the point that my mother would tease me: "Are you reading the future?" She wasn't entirely wrong; I was reading all the possibilities. To end something was to abandon it. "It's just coffee," Thomas kept pointing out.

But it was black.

"The paper?" my mother asked me on the way to the hospital. The word "paper" struggled in her goitre like a fish in a pelican's beak.

I'd heard her perfectly, but I asked her to say it again

so I could see the funny face she made and enjoy my just deserts. I felt like I was stealing something from existence. The paper-fish in my mother's throat was smaller than the first one but it still made me smile.

"Well?"

My mother was losing her patience, convinced that I'd forgotten it. She was afraid. And that was why I was annoyed with her. It was *my* fear, and this fear had no space for other people's fear. But as I looked at Thomas's smooth face, his grey eyes that, like my mother's, wanted to see the paper, I didn't have the heart to get angry and I pulled out the documents for the "ambulatory" operation.

I found the phrase rather bizarre, as if the operation would be happening in the middle of nowhere, in a hall-way, on the go; a surgeon would burst out, a headlamp stuck on his forehead, to fasten me to a trolley and tinker with my organs in the middle of the hospital's chaos. No, "ambulatory" simply meant that I could leave the hospital that same night, that, if all went well, I'd be back home the same night, a bandage around my head in the silence.

Once at the hospital, the glass door struck me as far more gleaming than last time. It opened automatically. We'd had our free will taken from us: the hospital was calling all the shots now. I was a bit of reality to be brought even more in line with reality.

With an implant, I might have 8000-hertz hearing, bringing me somewhat closer to the 15000 hertz that a hearing person my age might have, the speech therapist had told me.

In the hospital corridors leading to reception, the glass panes caught the reflection of my hearing aid cable, a tiny filament in the long hallway, and I thought of those fish that become blobs because of the pressure change as they are brought to the surface.

"Where's Anna?" I asked. "Why didn't Anna come?"

My paper was yawning in the gap between my legs. Thomas now had his rough-seas eyes; he set the paper on an empty seat, beside my mother's worried gaze. He closed his hands around my fingers, made a bouquet of them, focused on them; he drowned the question in this bouquet of fingernails that I'd already bitten to the quick. Then, looking apologetic, he said: "Forget about her, it's not important."

Everything went quickly: the white of the walls, the linoleum sticking to my soles, the smell of antiseptic and warm bandages and bleach. Once I reached the surgical suite, Thomas's and my mother's faces disappeared and then men in face masks appeared. The hair around my ear was shaved off before I lay down on the trolley. I started feeling cold in my untied hospital gown. I shut my eyes to forget the plaster ceiling and the fluorescent lights giving me goosebumps. Under my eyelids tensed by waiting, I saw Anna and the soldier with their tender gazes on me.

I felt the trolley's jolting. The air going by as I moved

216

caused my eyes to open, my skin to prickle. I was being wheeled into the operating room. I saw the fluorescent lights going by slowly, the hallways one after another. Then the light was different: I was in the operating room.

They fastened my arms and legs, the anaesthetist gave me the okay sign. He injected the liquid through the tube.

80

In my dark house, with a beaten-earth floor, only a few rays of light streak the walls. I can make out shapes, other people are shifting around, silhouettes in the dark. One last burst and the house cracks, the wind rushes through the gaps, the force of the wind immobilises my body, laying it out flat. The silhouettes close in jerkily, as if drunk, the momentum now gone. The gestures stop, the sounds disintegrate in the wind, an icy whistle enters my ear.

Muttering of drunk sobriquets
Jawbone chewing the Pyrénées
Ice cap left for dead
Overtone song of green Crocs
Avalanche of cups-and-balls.

Translator's Acknowledgements

I was far younger than Louise F. when I got a cochlear implant in 1995. This translation may have been three months in the doing, but the truth is that it was three decades in the making.

As I faced down the list of heard and misheard words that, in English, begins "woman, lemon, boulder", it was deeply moving to enlist Beverly Fears, the audiologist who originally programmed my implant, and who had me do that same test countless times since, in recreating all the phonemes and meanings of the list in English.

For the text of the fictional *Anarchist Neuroscience Review*, which is drawn from real-life research, it tickled me to ask one of my best friends from college, Rachel Caplan, now a practising neurologist, to make it ring true in translation.

For the puns and misunderstandings festooning this text, a lifetime of lip-reading made most of those easy work. For the trickiest ones, Robin Munby and Maddy Robinson sparked the perfect solutions.

I am delighted to call Joachim Schnerf at Grasset and Katie Dublinski at Graywolf dear friends; I owe them a debt of gratitude for entrusting me to turn *Les Méduses n'ont pas d'oreilles* into *Jellyfish Have No Ears*. Katharina Bielenberg and Allie Mayers at MacLehose, likewise, were dream collaborators for the British edition. Sigrid Rausing, Eleanor Chandler, and especially Lucy Diver were invaluable allies as the book's first few sections were excerpted in what was, for all three of them, the final issue of *Granta* they edited.

On the production side, the final book owes so much to being typeset by the team at Bookmobile, copyedited by Lynn Marasco and proofread by Jordan Koluch in the US; and to being typeset by Susan Wightman and proofread by Rita Winter Gesche Ipsen in the UK.

It is not often that I have the good fortune to bring a book into English at the same time that other translators are ferrying it into other languages. To this book's Dutch translator, Carlijn Brouwer, and to the many other translators whose questions Adèle shared with me, it is a pleasure to call you *camarades d'absourdité*.

And of course this book itself would not exist without Adèle Rosenfeld, whose heart comes through in its every sentence and even word. Adèle, aucun mot ne peut exprimer comment ce livre m'émeut et m'a été d'un grand secours lorsque j'en avais besoin. Que ce « nouvel être vivant » donne à ton écriture une vie aussi immortelle que celle d'une méduse.

And to my parents, Lois and Dave Zuckerman, who made the nerve-wracking decision all those years ago so I wouldn't have to.

ADÈLE ROSENFELD was born in in Paris in 1986 and has worked in publishing for the last ten years. Alongside her work, she has developed a number of writing projects. Her first novel, *Jellyfish Have No Ears*, was shortlisted for the prestigious Prix Goncourt du Premier Roman 2022.

JEFFREY ZUCKERMAN is a translator of French, including the Mauritian novelists Ananda Devi, Shenaz Patel, and Carl de Souza. A graduate of Yale University, he has been a finalist for the PEN Translation Prize and the French-American Foundation Translation Prize, and a winner of the French Voices Grand Prize. In 2020 he was named a Chevalier de l'Ordre des Arts et des Lettres by the French government.